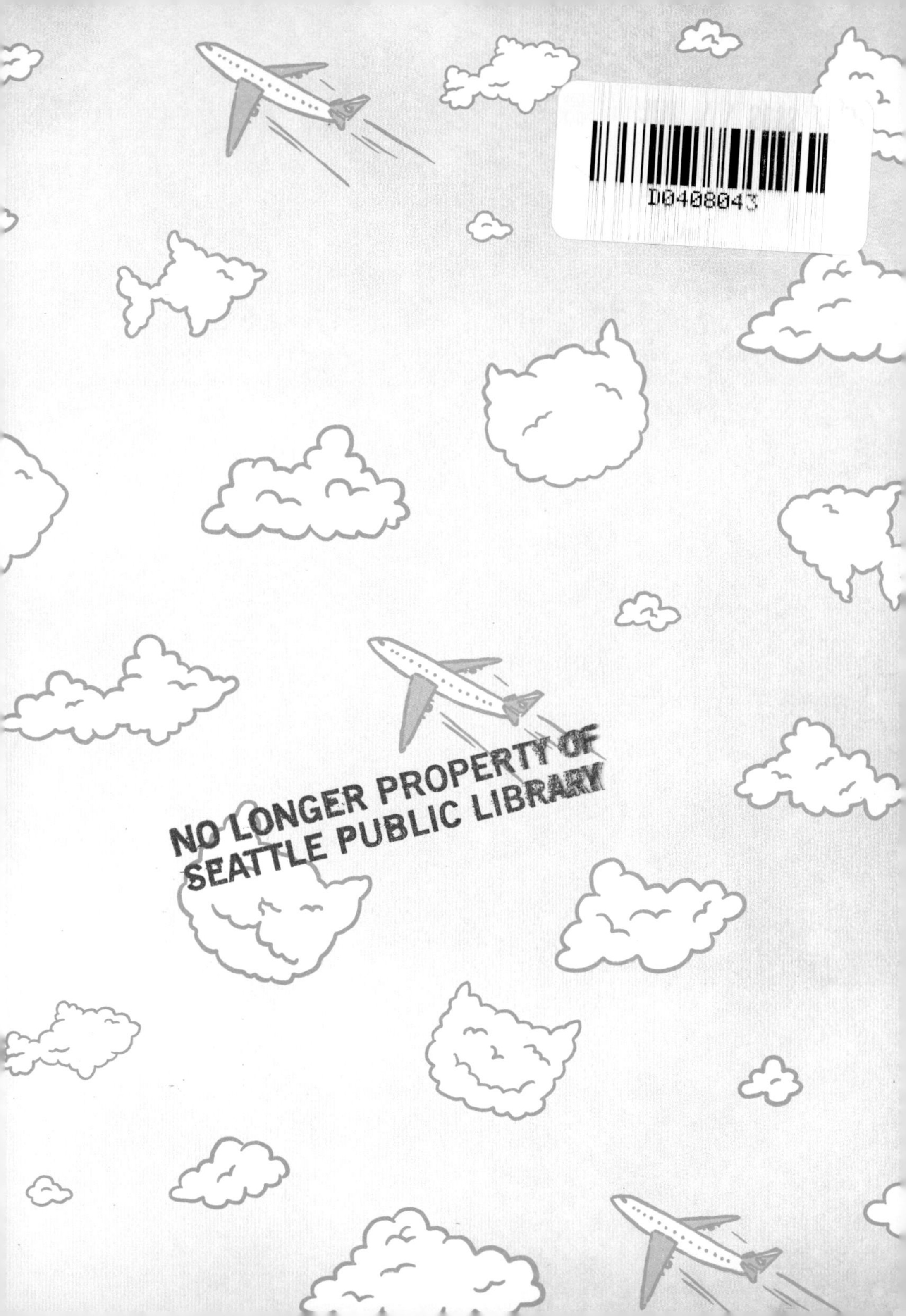

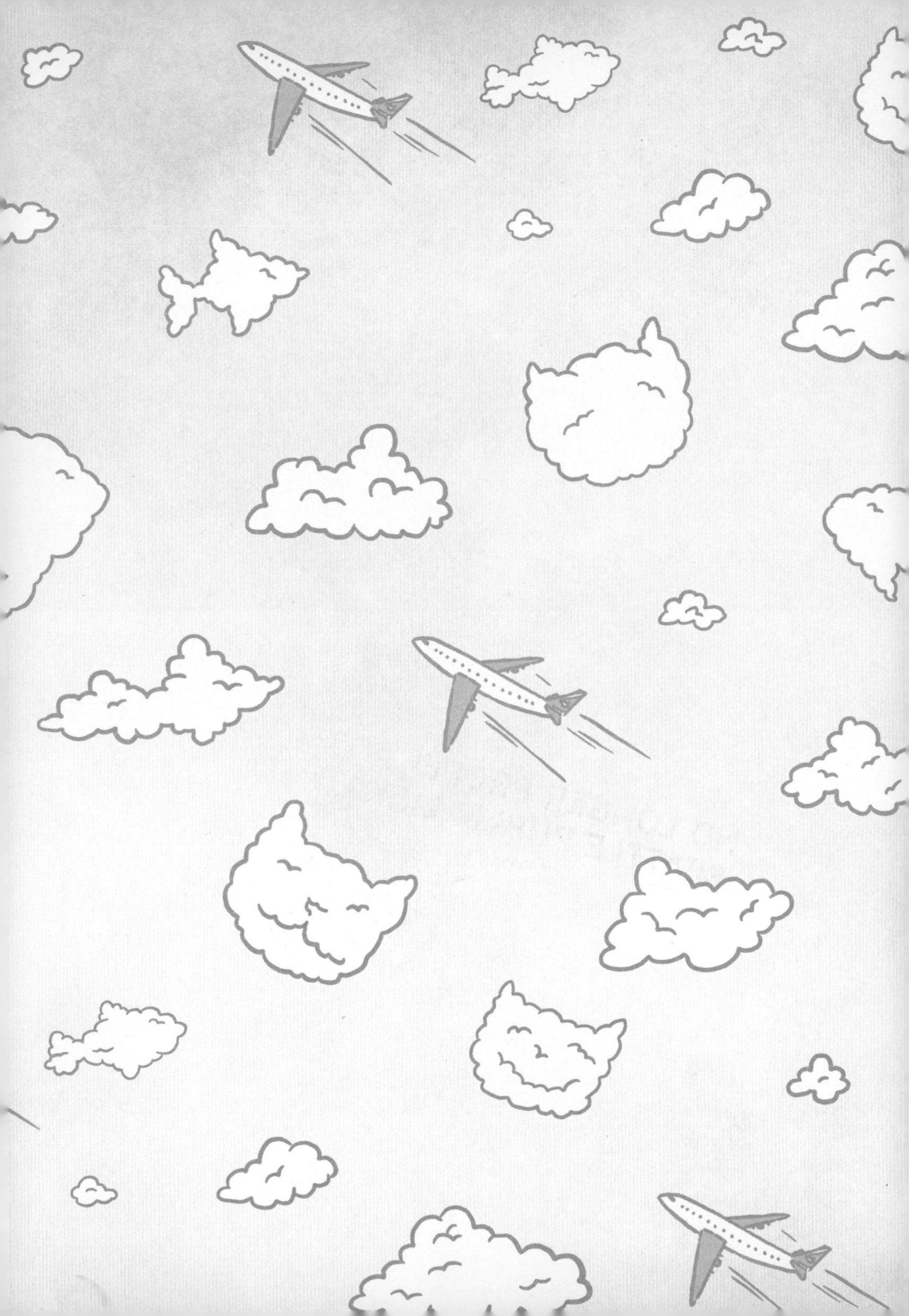

A CATSTRONAUTS KITTEN ADVENTURE

WAFFLES AND PANCAKE

FLIGHT OR FRIGHT

A CATSTRONAUTS KITTEN ADVENTURE

WAFFLES AND PANCAKE

FLIGHT OR FRIGHT

DREW BROCKINGTON

LB

Little, Brown and Company

New York • Boston

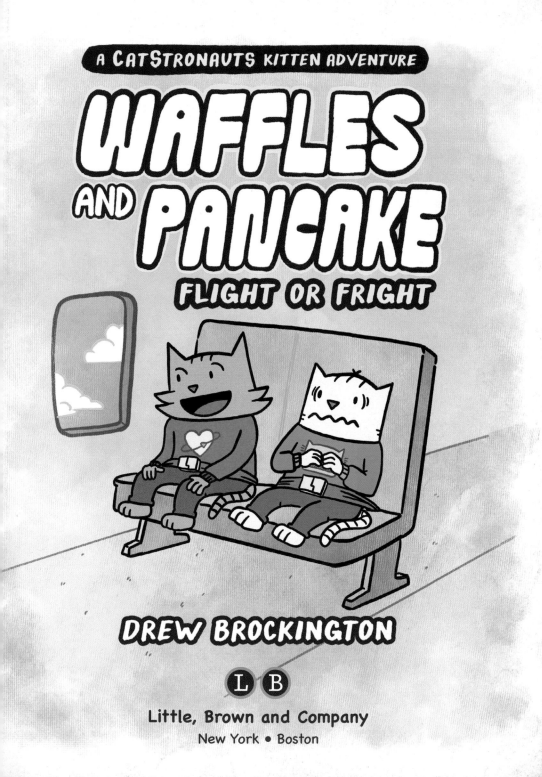

About This Book

This book was edited by Rachel Poloski and Liz Kossnar and designed by Ching N. Chan. The production was supervised by Kimberly Stella, and the production editor was Jake Regier. The text was set in Colby, and the display type was created by Drew Brockington.

Little, Brown and Company
Hachette Book Group
1290 Avenue of the Americas, New York, NY 10104
Visit us at LBYR.com

First Edition: June 2022

Little, Brown and Company is a division of Hachette Book Group, Inc.
The Little, Brown name and logo are trademarks of Hachette Book Group, Inc.

The publisher is not responsible for websites (or their content) that are not owned by the publisher.

Library of Congress Cataloging-in-Publication Data
Names: Brockington, Drew, author, illustrator.
Title: Flight or fright / by Drew Brockington.
Description: First edition. | New York ; Boston : Little, Brown and Company, 2022. | Series: Waffles and Pancake | Audience: Ages 6–9. | Summary: Waffles, Pancake, and Mom-Cat go to visit Gramps and Grammers, but this is the kittens' first time flying on an airplane, and Waffles is a little nervous.
Identifiers: LCCN 2021031462 | ISBN 9780316500449 (paper over board) | ISBN 9780316500432 (ebook) | ISBN 9780316500463 (ebook) | ISBN 9780316500470 (ebook)
Subjects: CYAC: Graphic novels. | Fear—Fiction. | Airplanes—Fiction. | Flight—Fiction. | Cats—Fiction. | Brothers and sisters—Fiction. | LCGFT: Graphic novels.
Classification: LCC PZ7.7.B76 Fl 2022 | DDC 741.5/973—dc23
LC record available at https://lccn.loc.gov/2021031462

ISBNs: 978-0-316-50044-9 (paper over board), 978-0-316-50043-2 (ebook), 978-0-316-50046-3 (ebook), 978-0-316-50047-0 (ebook)

PRINTED IN CHINA

APS

10 9 8 7 6 5 4 3 2 1

FOR SIMON

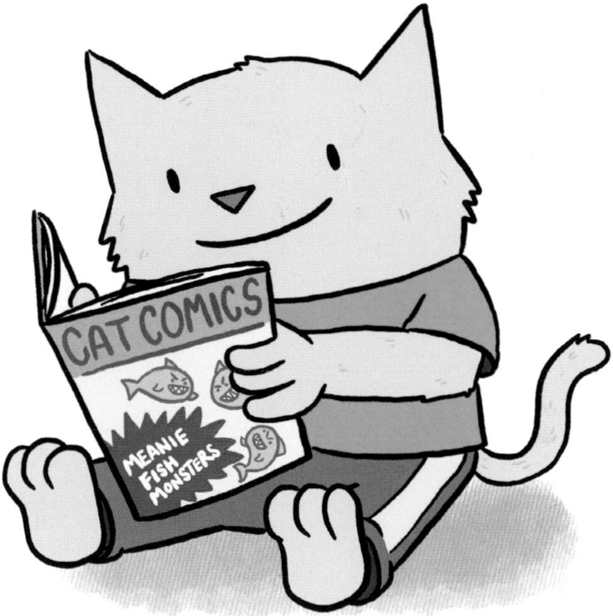
CAT COMICS
MEANIE FISH MONSTERS

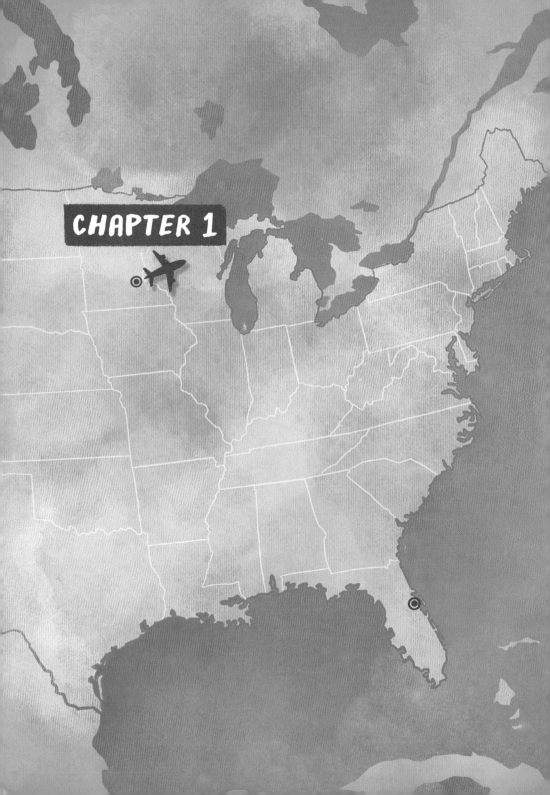

CHAPTER 1

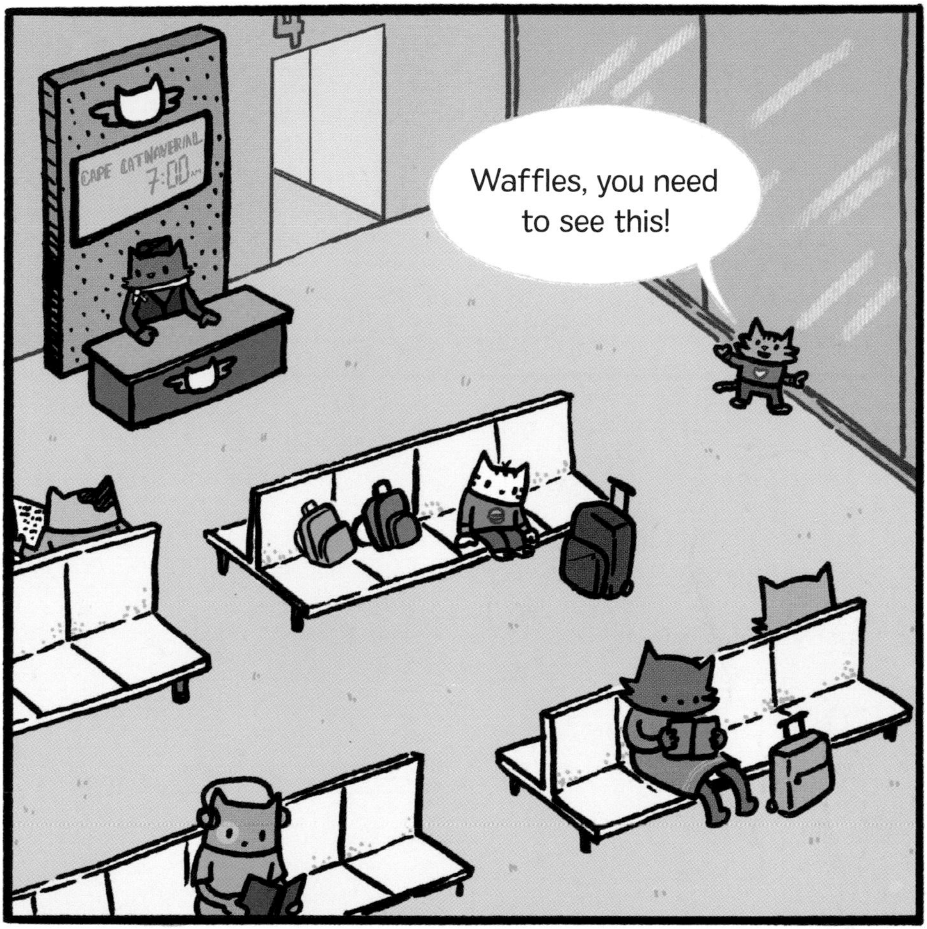
CAPE CATNAVERAL
7:00
Waffles, you need to see this!

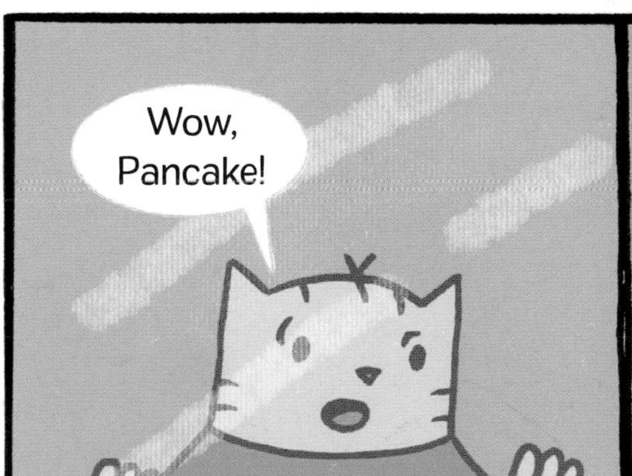
Wow, Pancake!

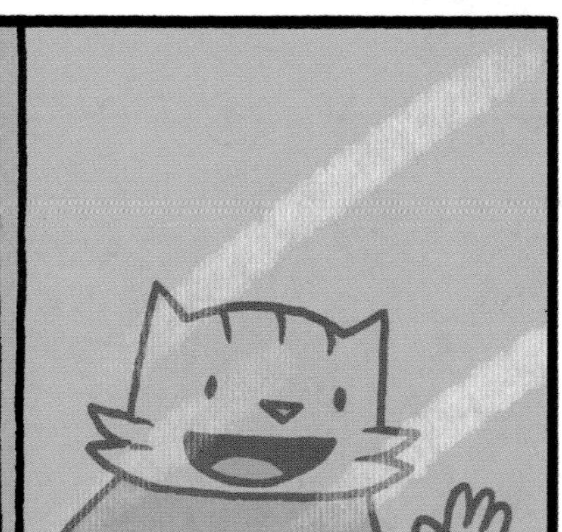

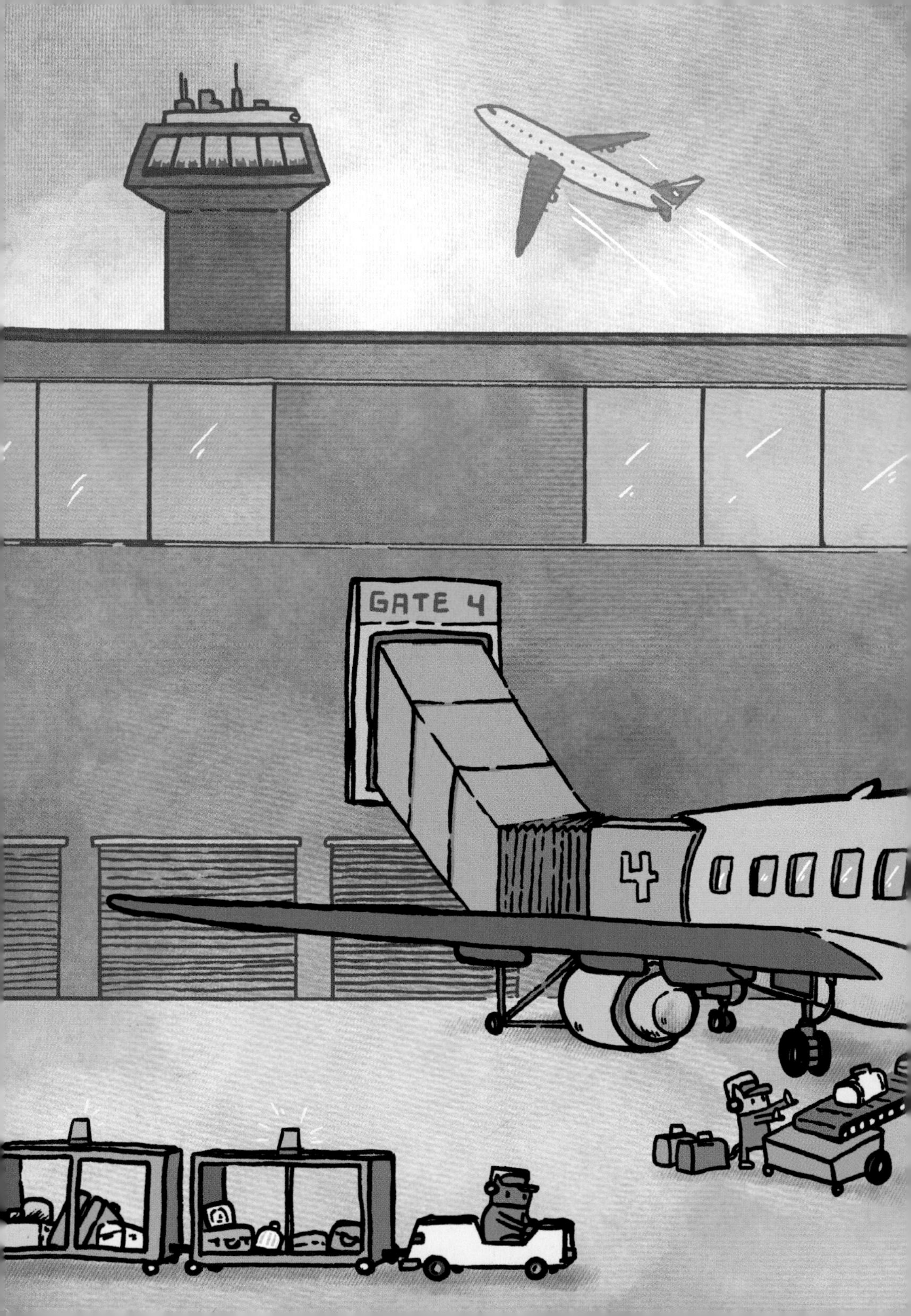
GATE 4
4

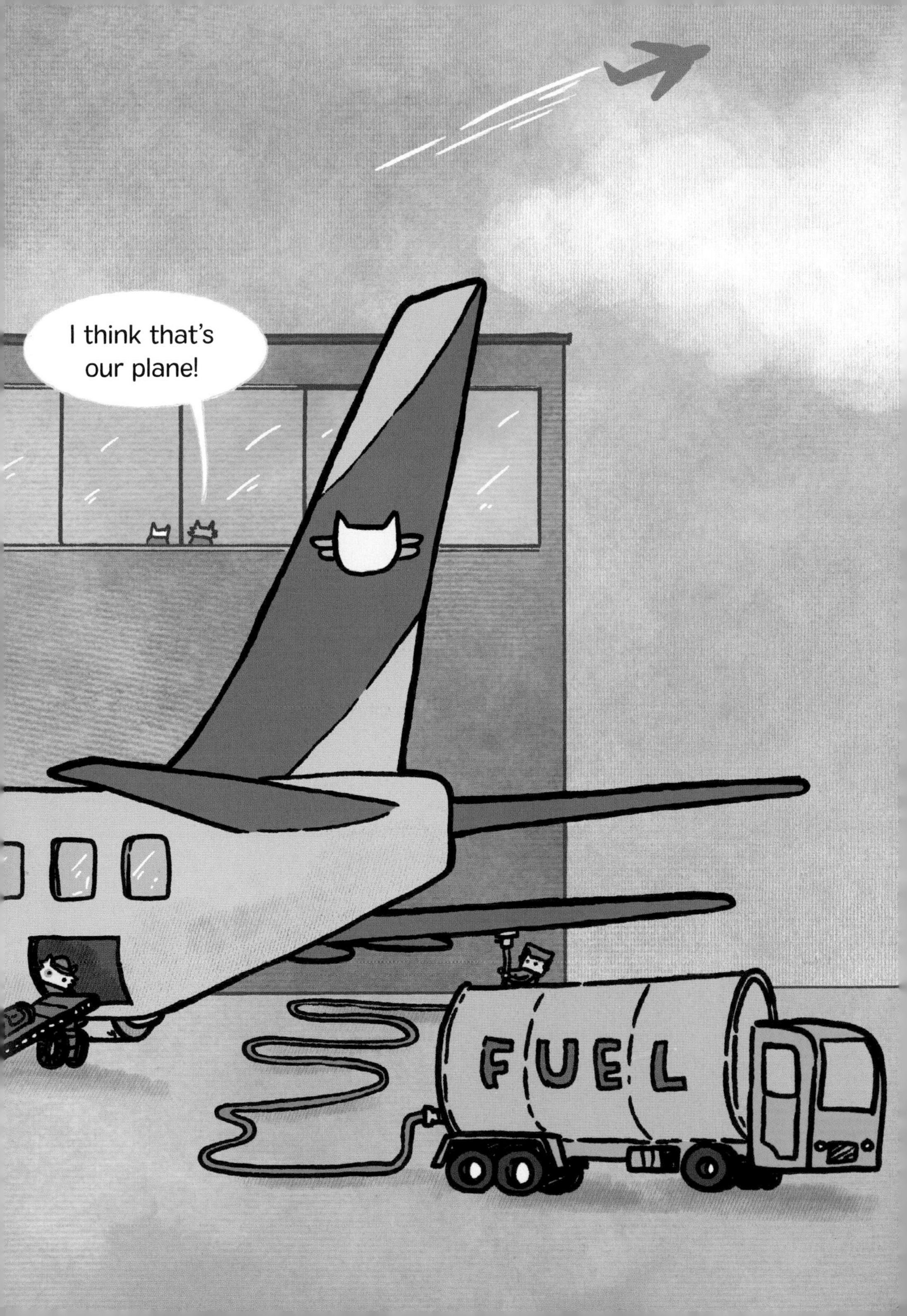
I think that's our plane!
FUEL

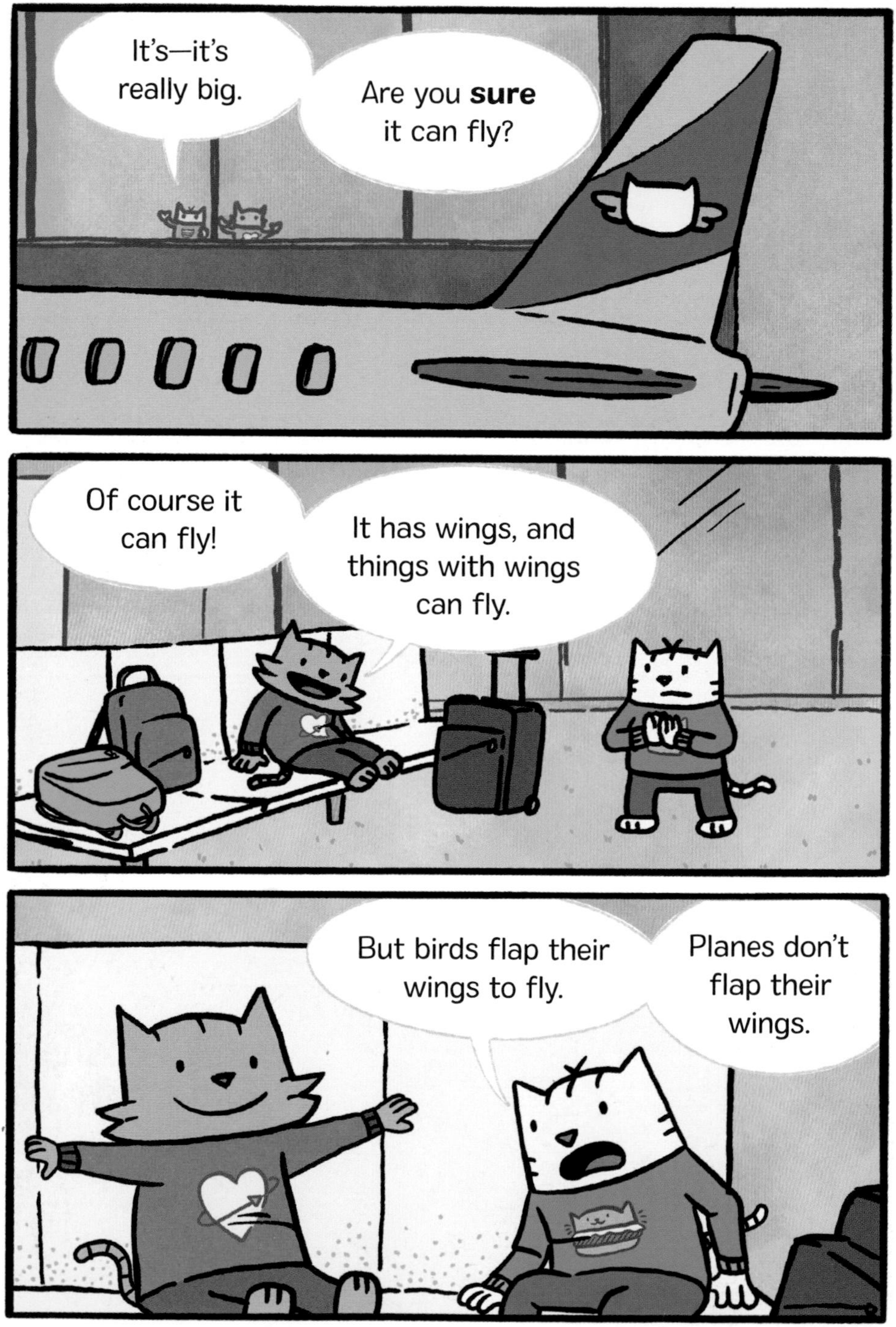
It's—it's really big.
Are you **sure** it can fly?
Of course it can fly!
It has wings, and things with wings can fly.
But birds flap their wings to fly.
Planes don't flap their wings.

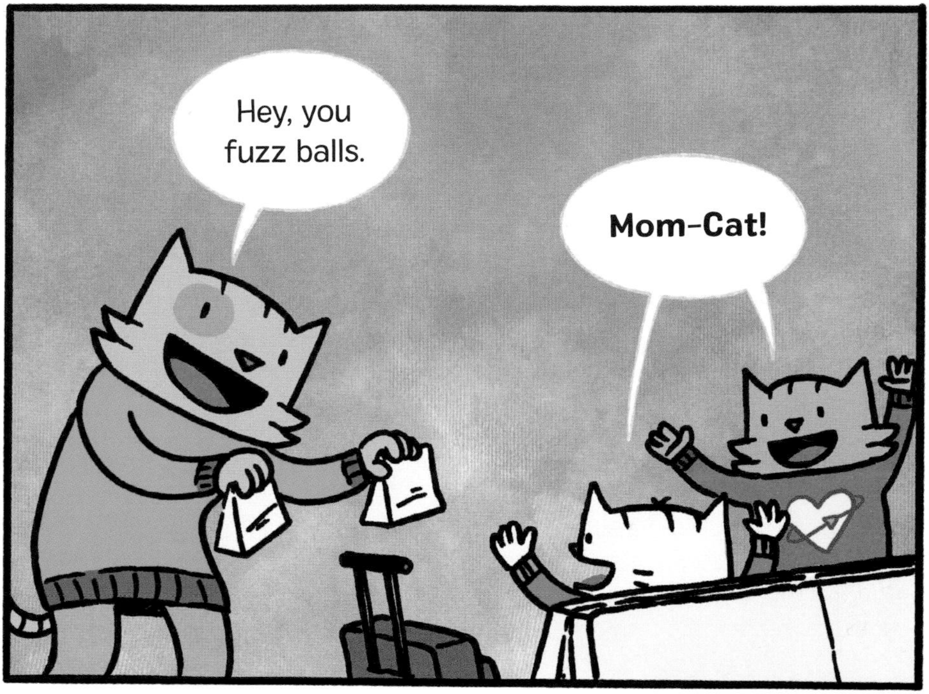
Hey, you
fuzz balls.
Mom-Cat!

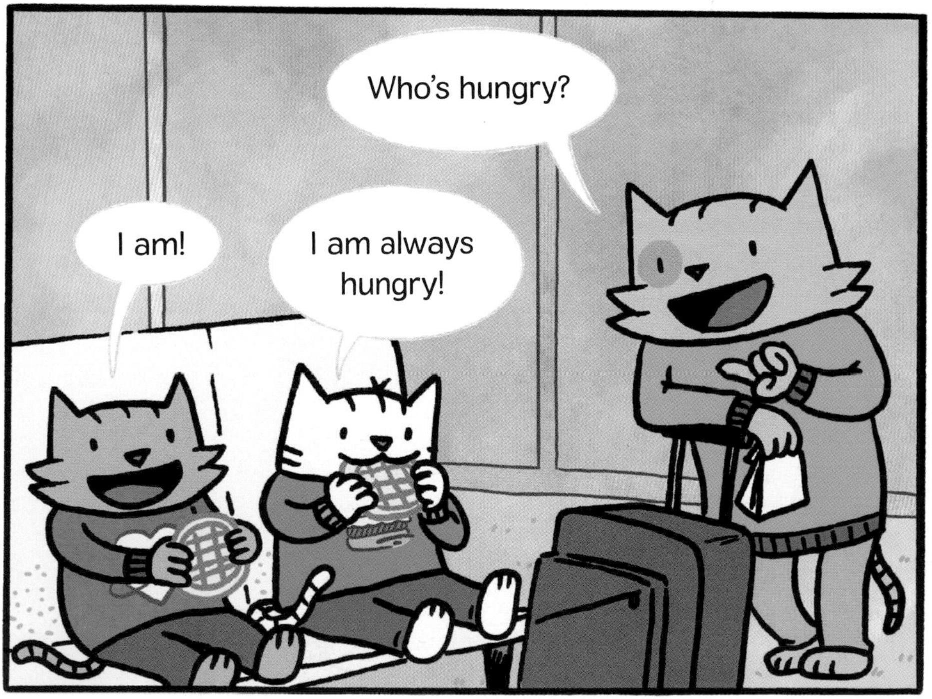
Who's hungry?
I am!
I am always
hungry!

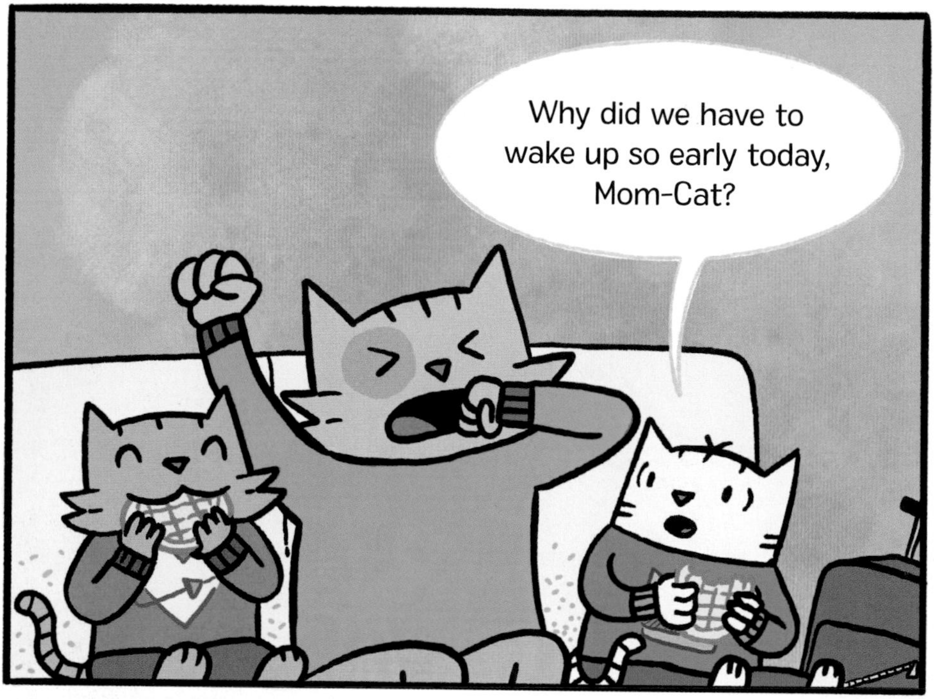
Why did we have to wake up so early today, Mom-Cat?

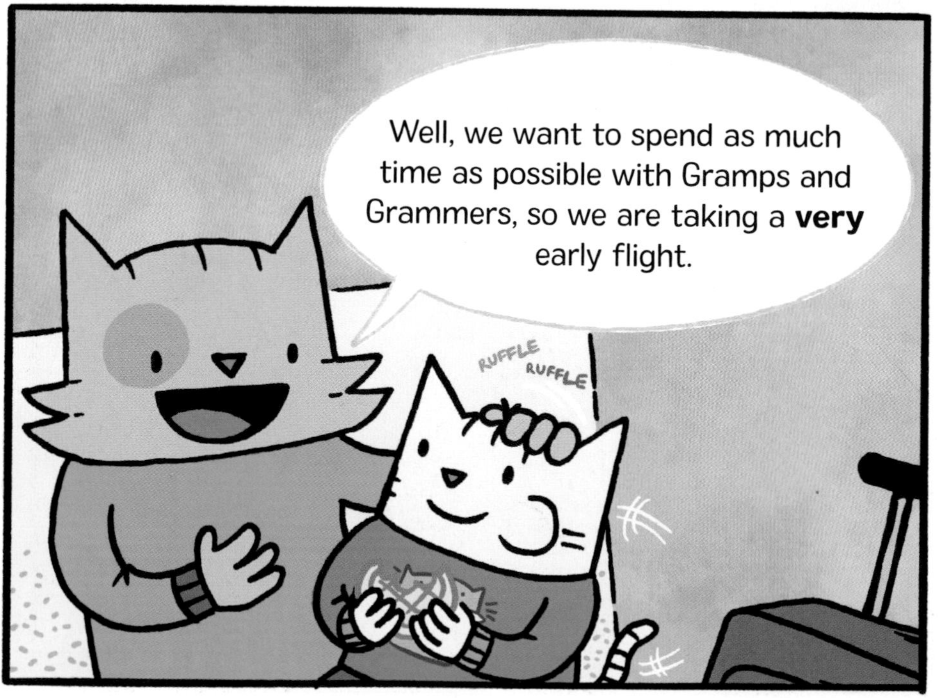
Well, we want to spend as much time as possible with Gramps and Grammers, so we are taking a **very** early flight.
RUFFLE RUFFLE

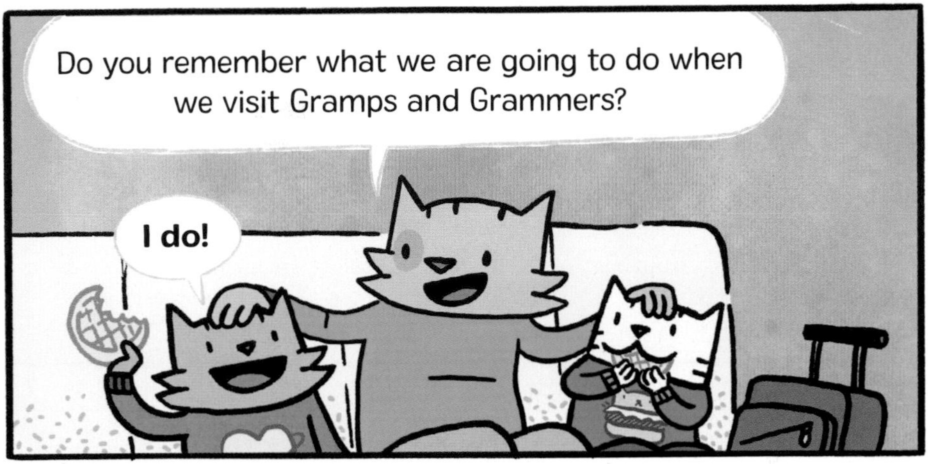
Do you remember what we are going to do when we visit Gramps and Grammers?
I do!

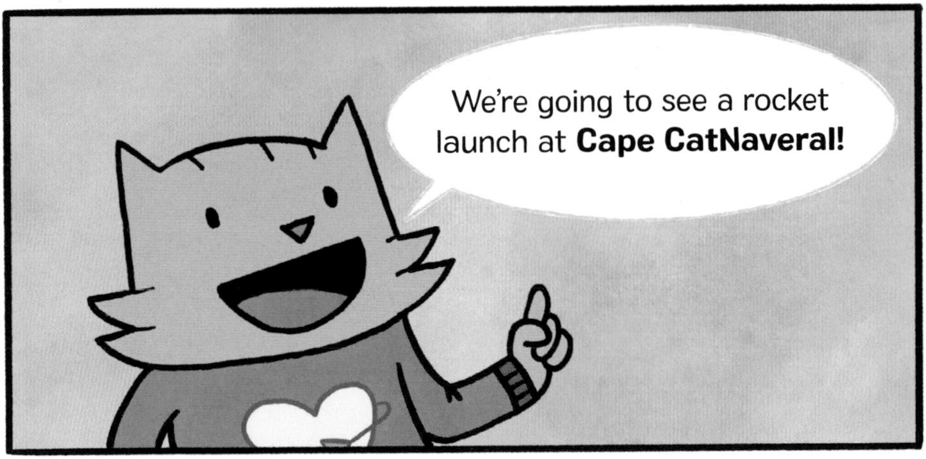
We're going to see a rocket launch at **Cape CatNaveral!**

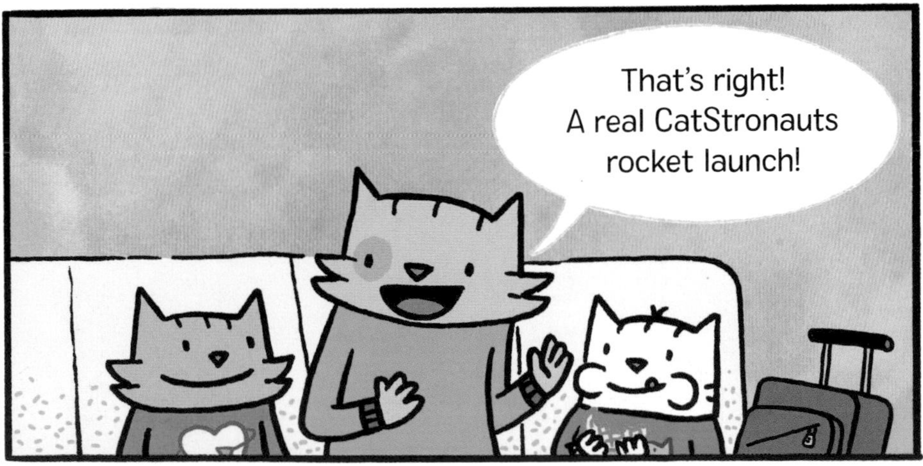
That's right! A real CatStronauts rocket launch!

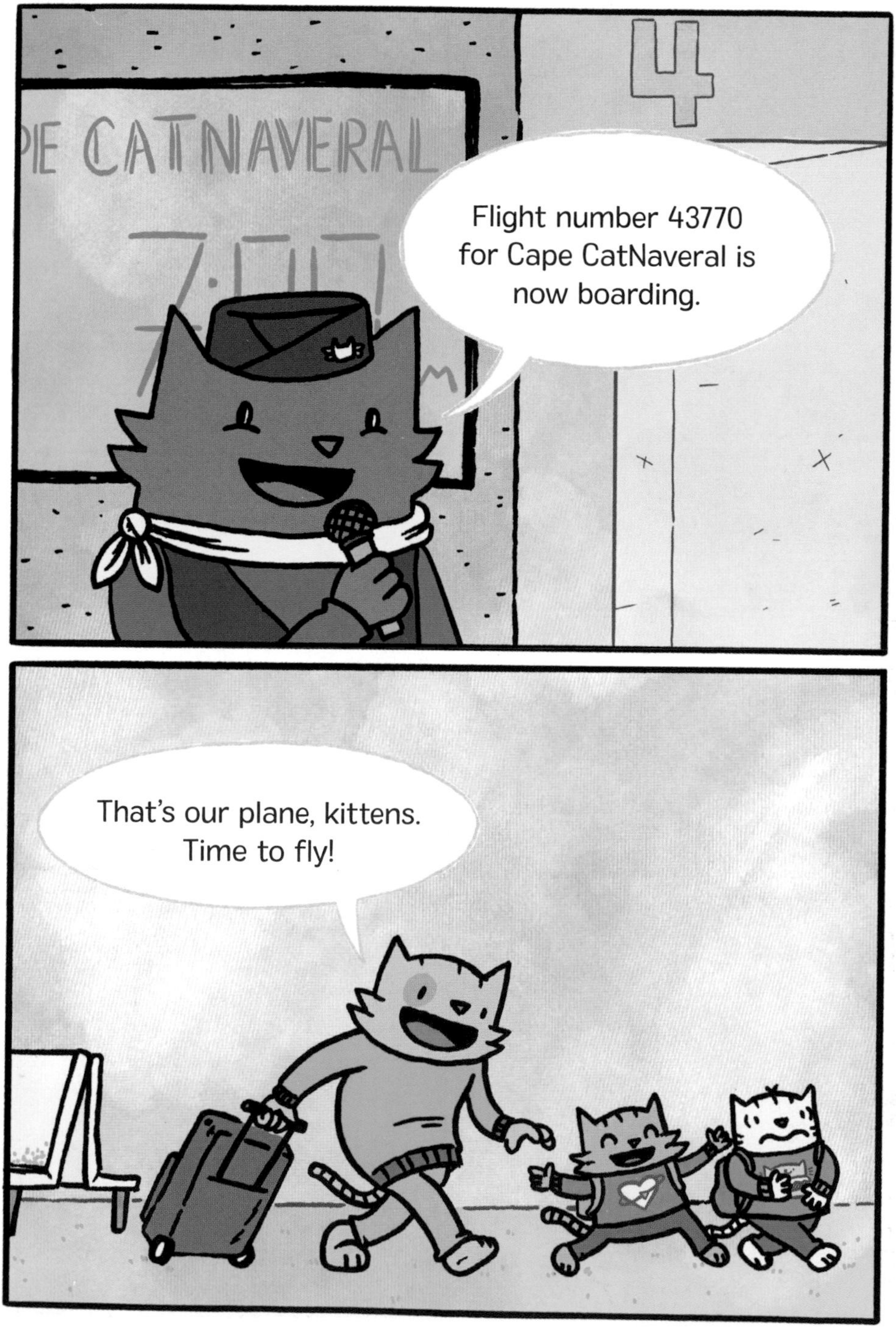

PE CATNAVERAL
4
Flight number 43770 for Cape CatNaveral is now boarding.
That's our plane, kittens. Time to fly!

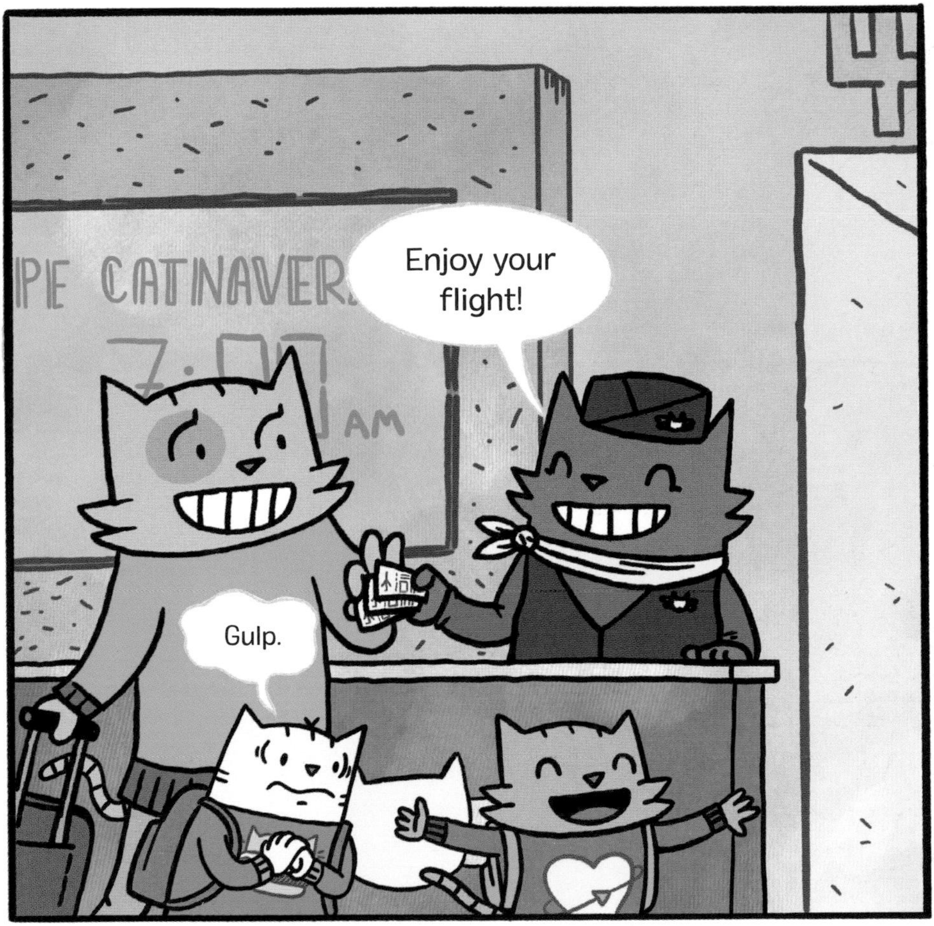
PE CATNAVER
7:00 AM
Enjoy your flight!
Gulp.

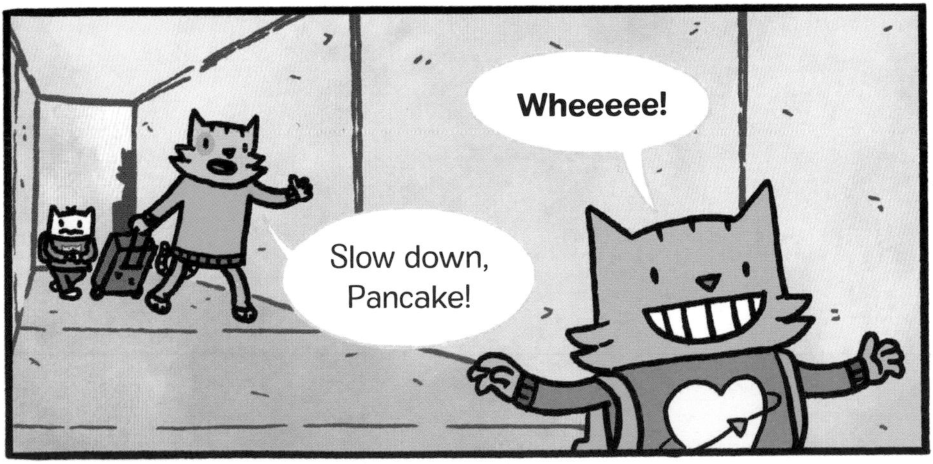
Wheeeee!
Slow down, Pancake!

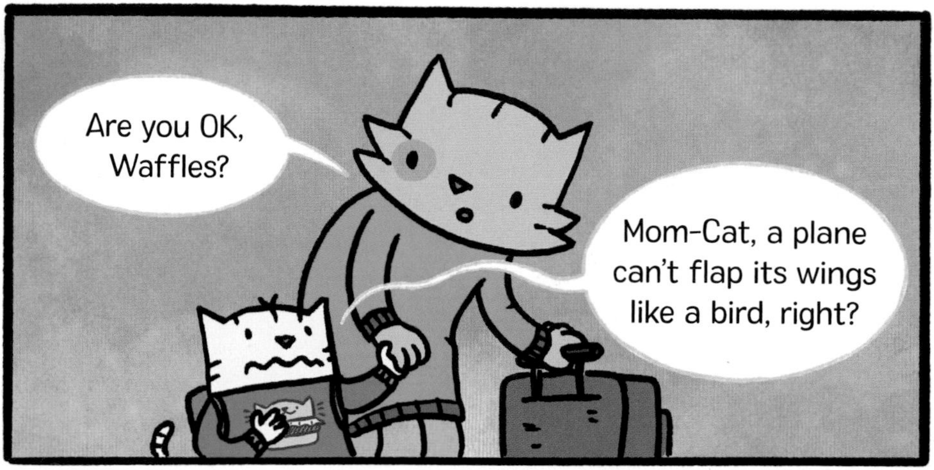
Are you OK, Waffles?
Mom-Cat, a plane can't flap its wings like a bird, right?

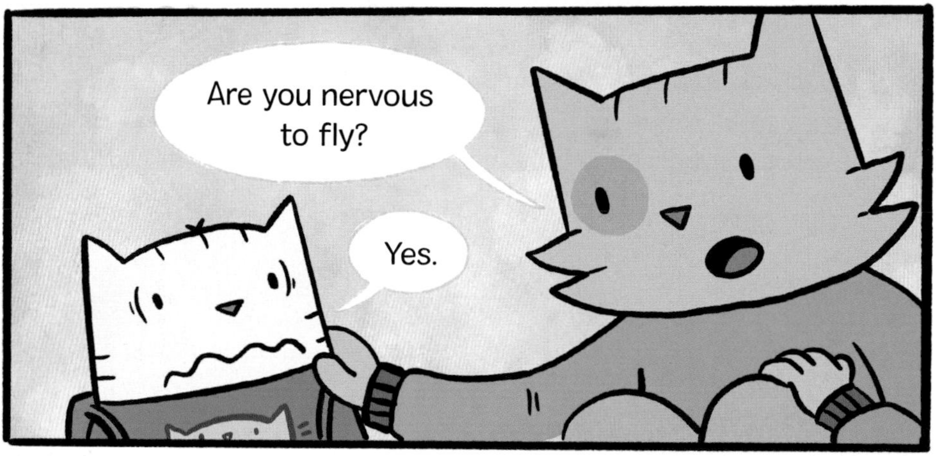
Are you nervous to fly?
Yes.

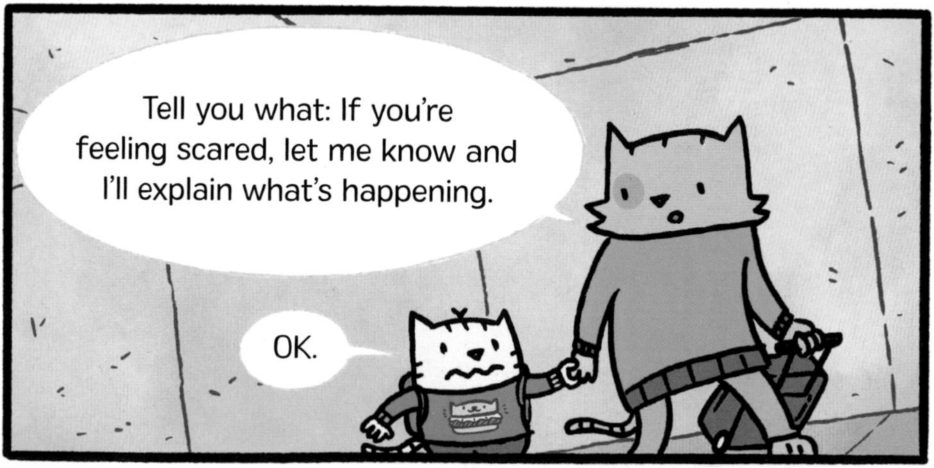
Tell you what: If you're feeling scared, let me know and I'll explain what's happening.
OK.

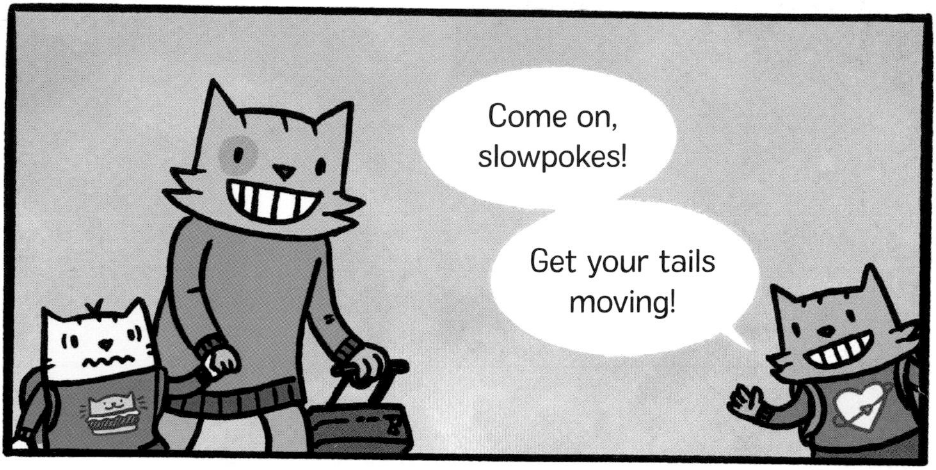
Come on, slowpokes!
Get your tails moving!

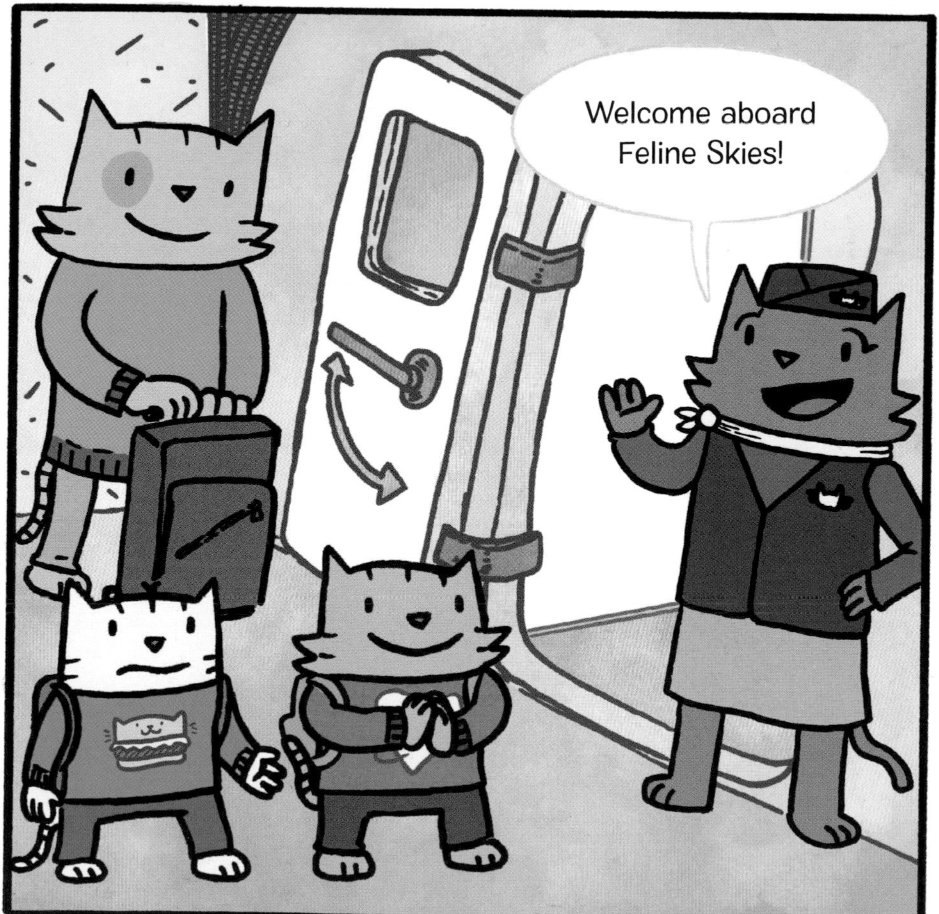
Welcome aboard Feline Skies!

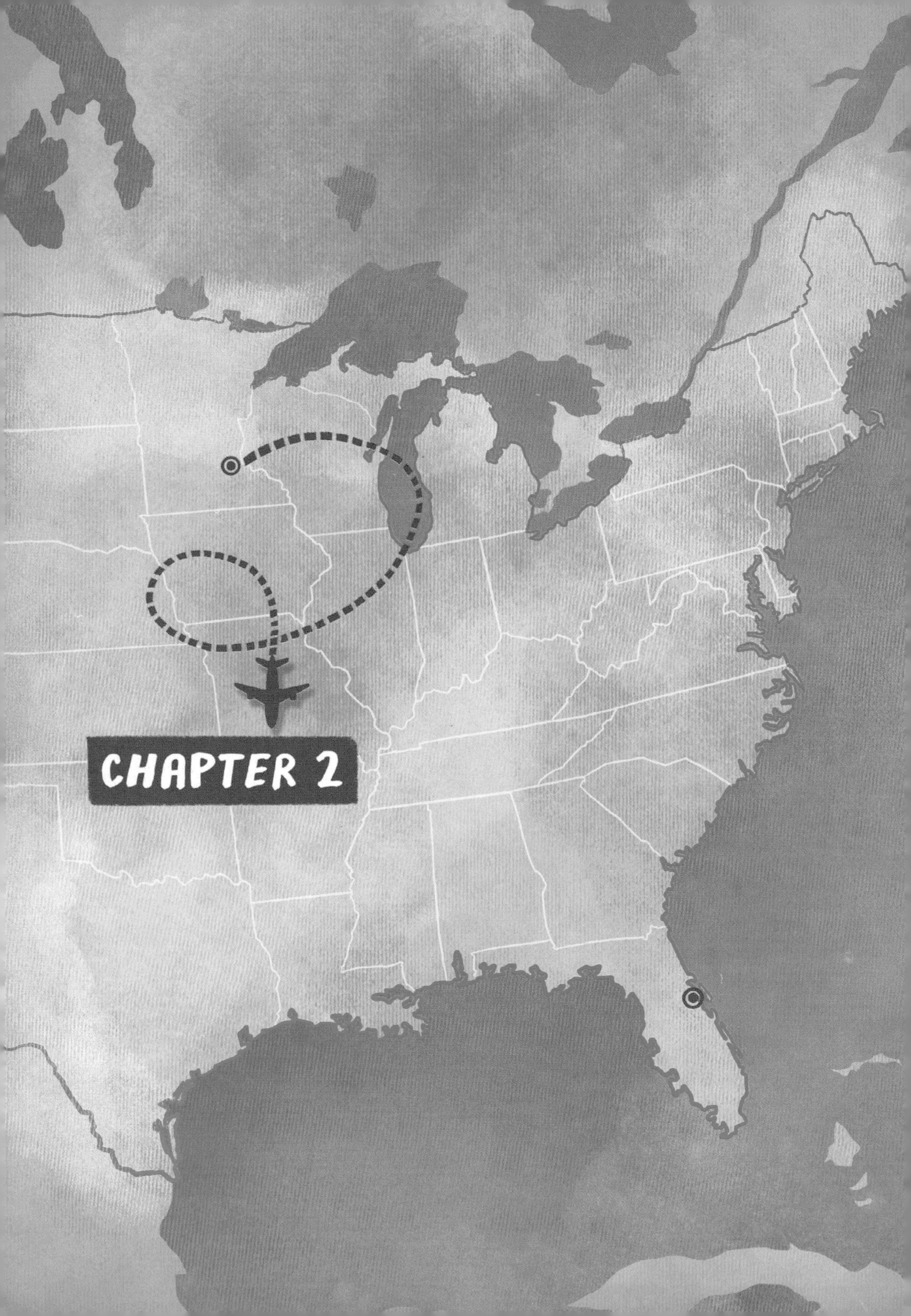

CHAPTER 2

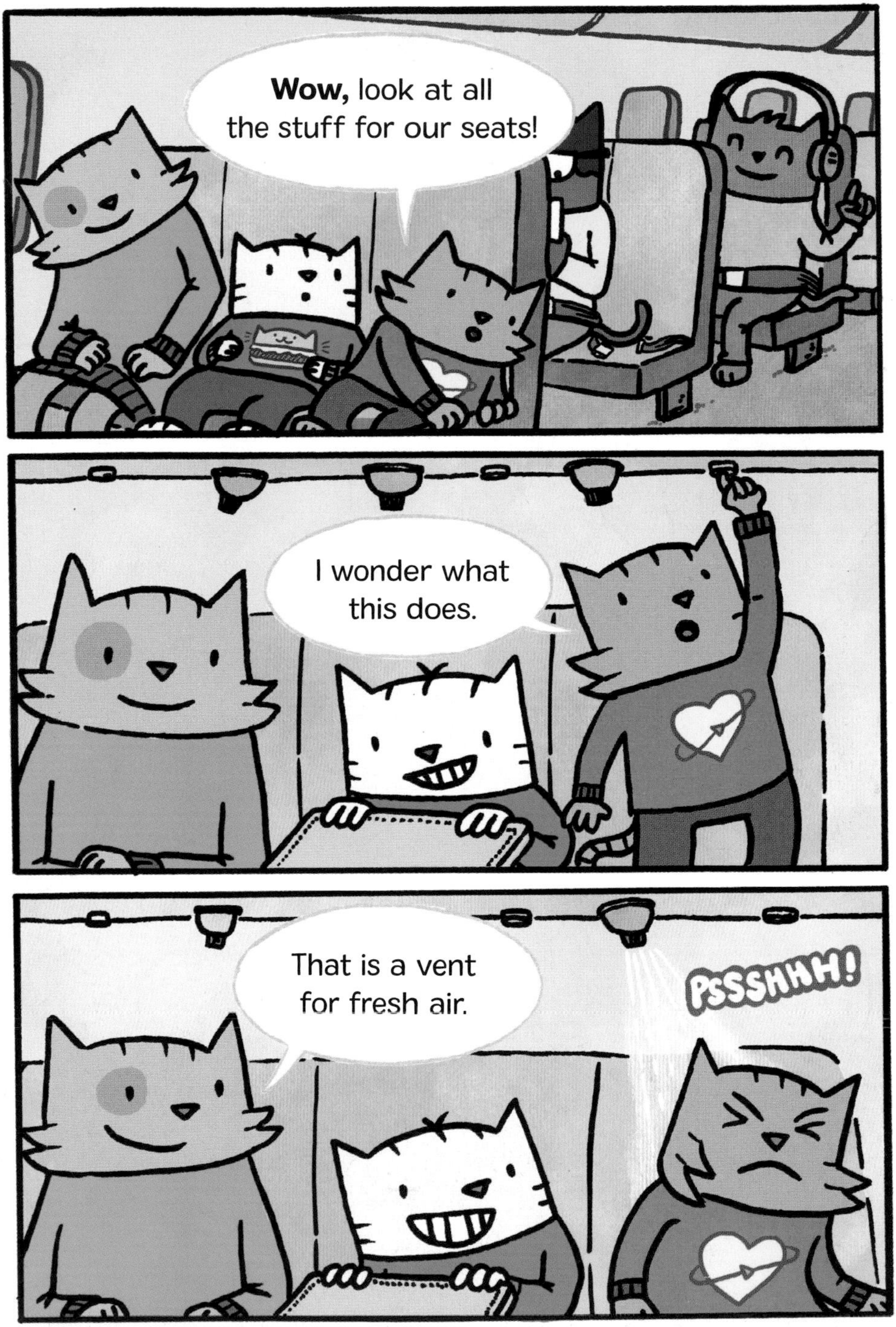
Wow, look at all the stuff for our seats!
I wonder what this does.
That is a vent for fresh air.
PSSSHHH!

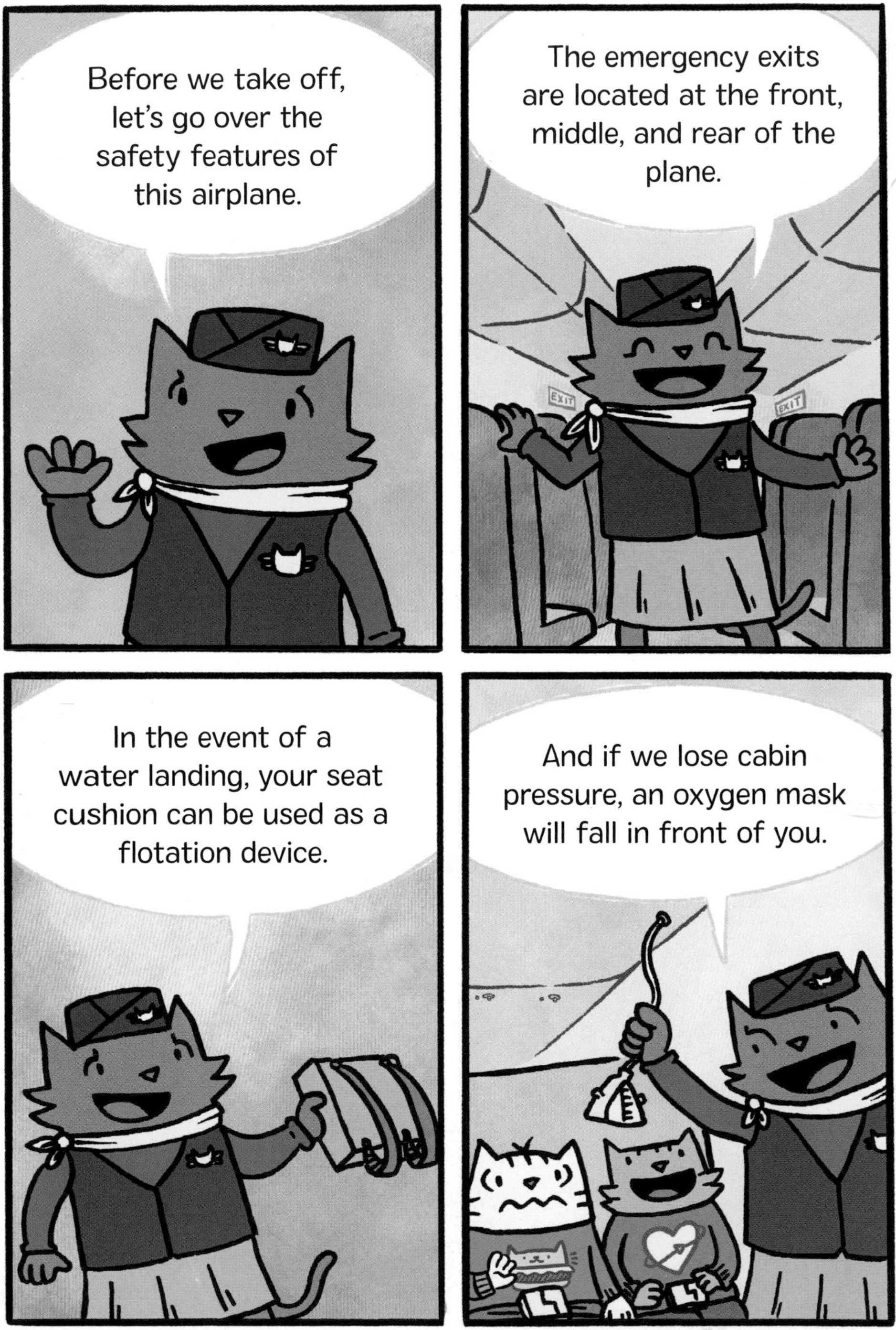
Before we take off, let's go over the safety features of this airplane.
The emergency exits are located at the front, middle, and rear of the plane.
EXIT
EXIT
In the event of a water landing, your seat cushion can be used as a flotation device.
And if we lose cabin pressure, an oxygen mask will fall in front of you.

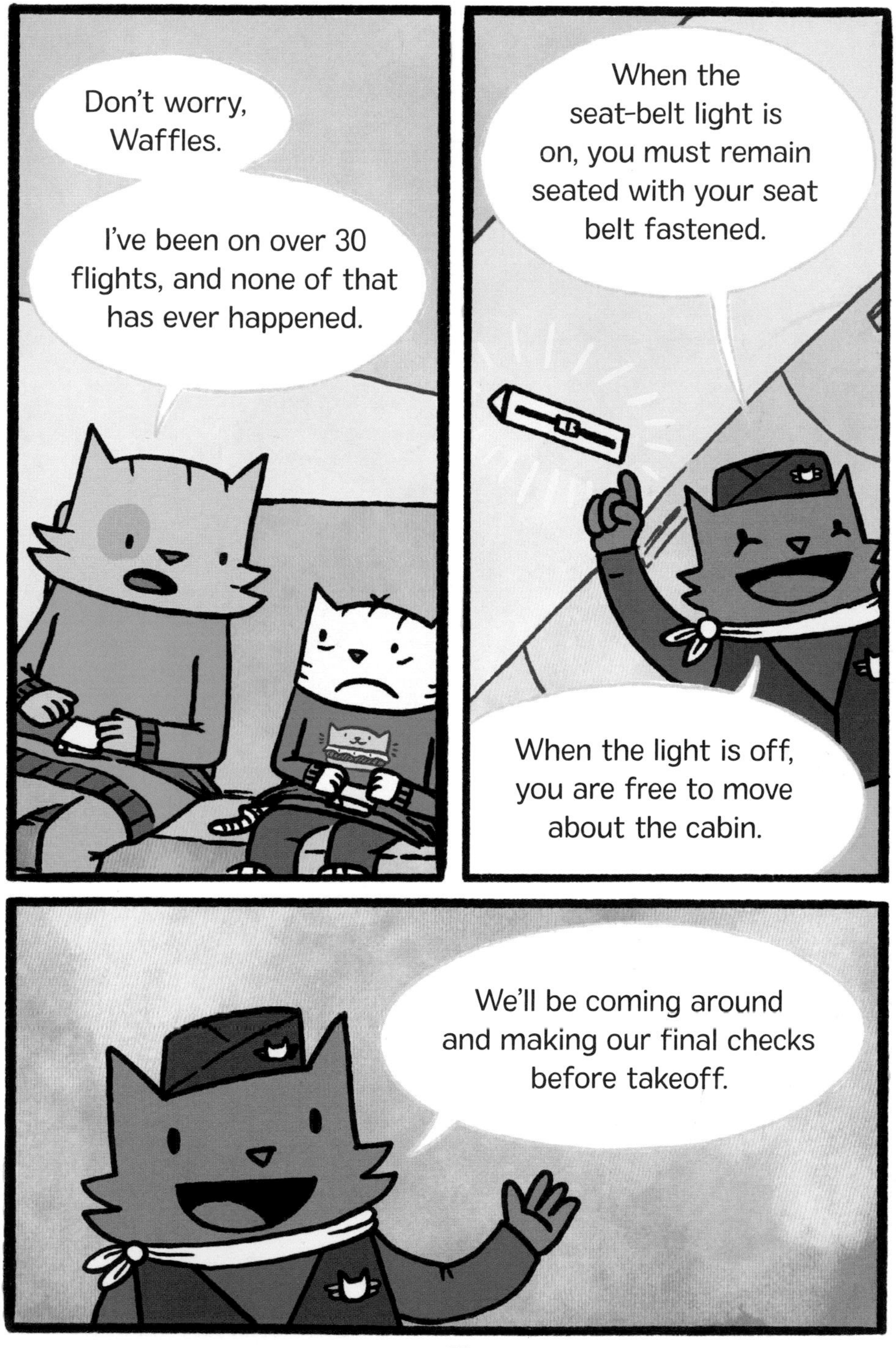
Don't worry, Waffles.
I've been on over 30 flights, and none of that has ever happened.
When the seat-belt light is on, you must remain seated with your seat belt fastened.
When the light is off, you are free to move about the cabin.
We'll be coming around and making our final checks before takeoff.

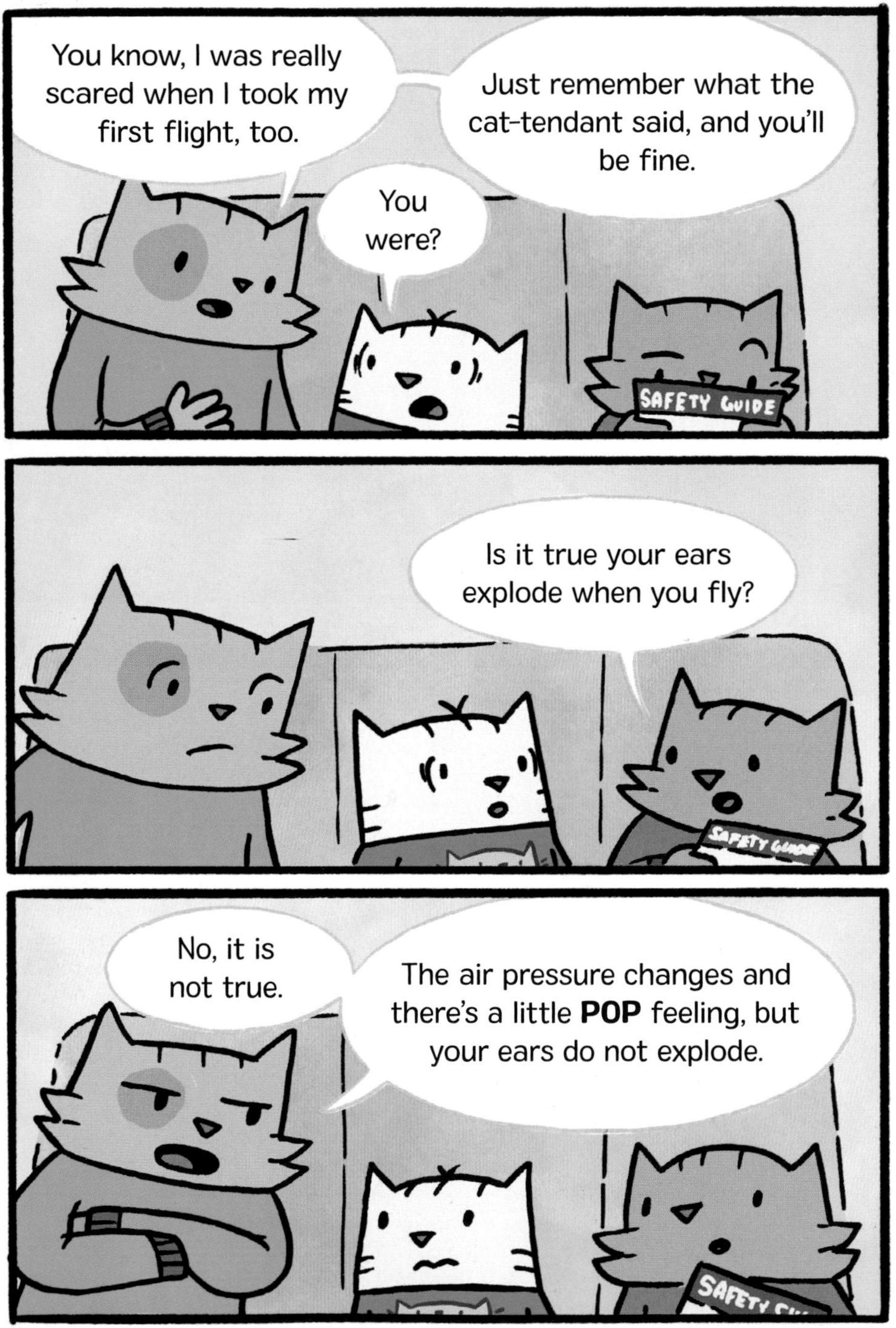
You know, I was really scared when I took my first flight, too.
You were?
Just remember what the cat-tendant said, and you'll be fine.
SAFETY GUIDE
Is it true your ears explode when you fly?
SAFETY GUIDE
No, it is not true.
The air pressure changes and there's a little **POP** feeling, but your ears do not explode.

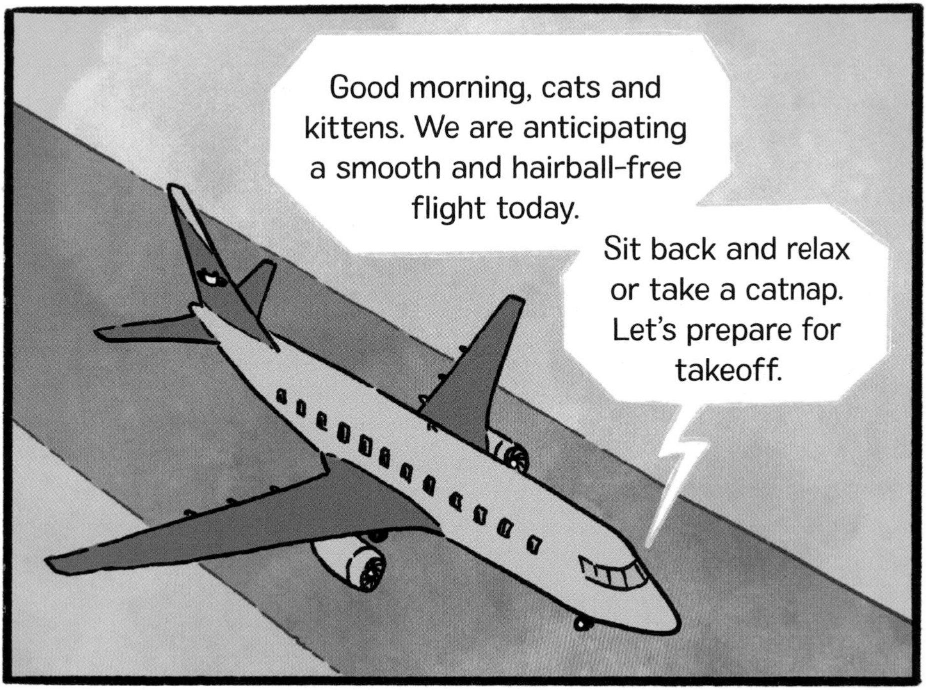
Good morning, cats and kittens. We are anticipating a smooth and hairball-free flight today.
Sit back and relax or take a catnap. Let's prepare for takeoff.

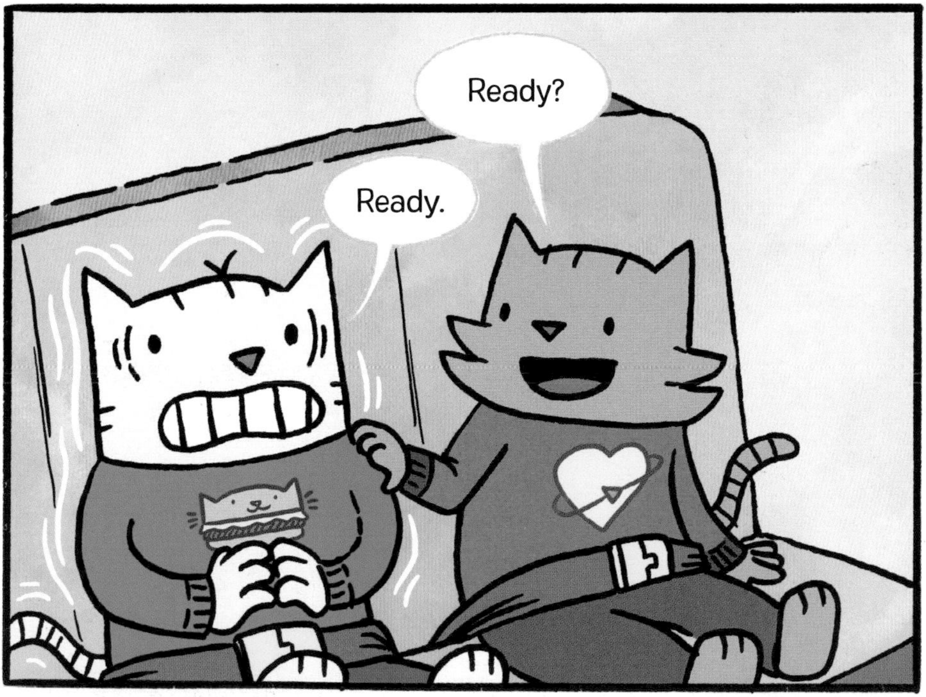
Ready?
Ready.

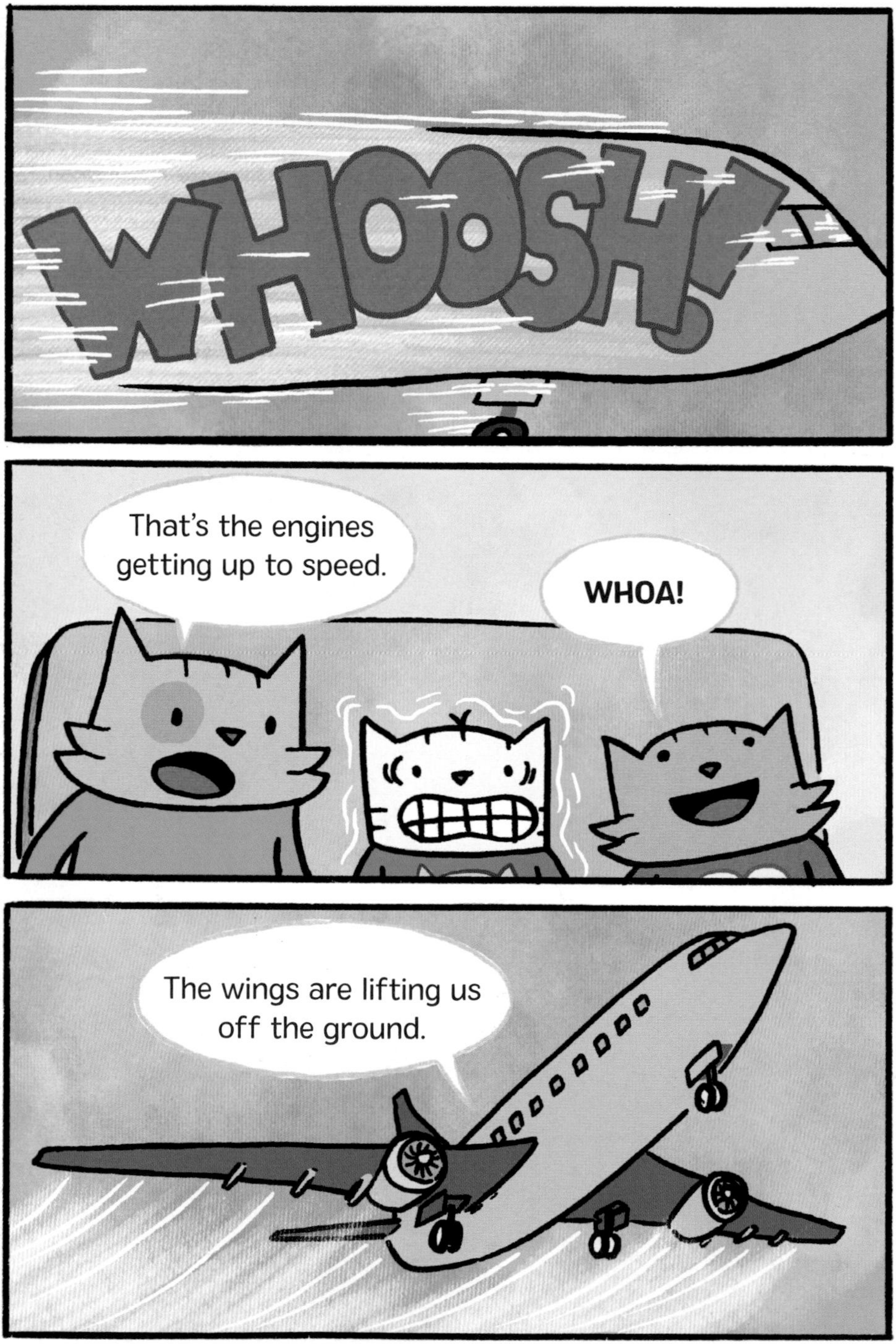
WHOOSH!
That's the engines getting up to speed.
WHOA!
The wings are lifting us off the ground.

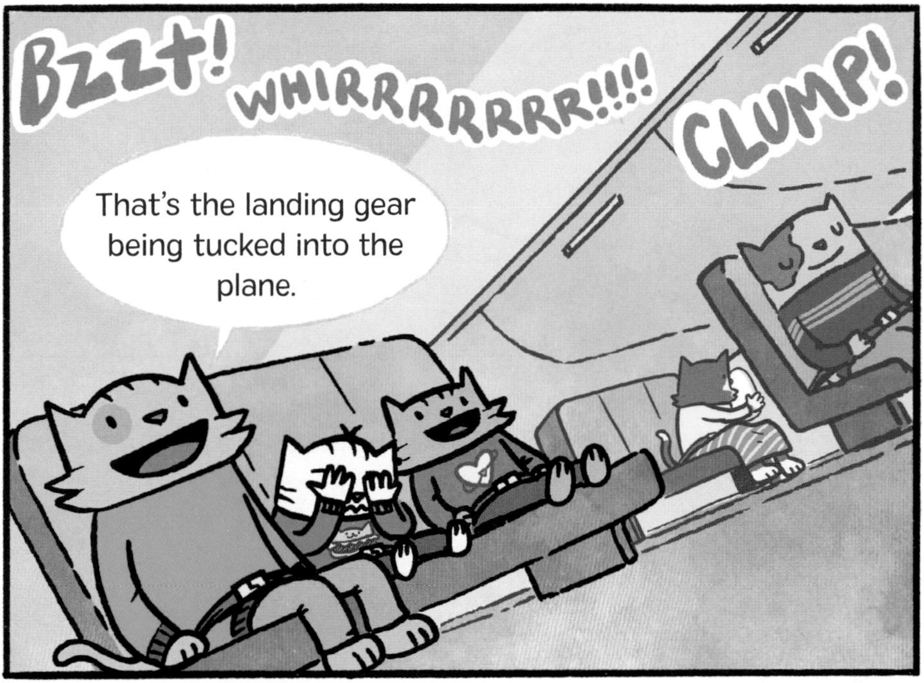
BZZT!
WHIRRRRRRRR!!!!
CLUMP!
That's the landing gear being tucked into the plane.

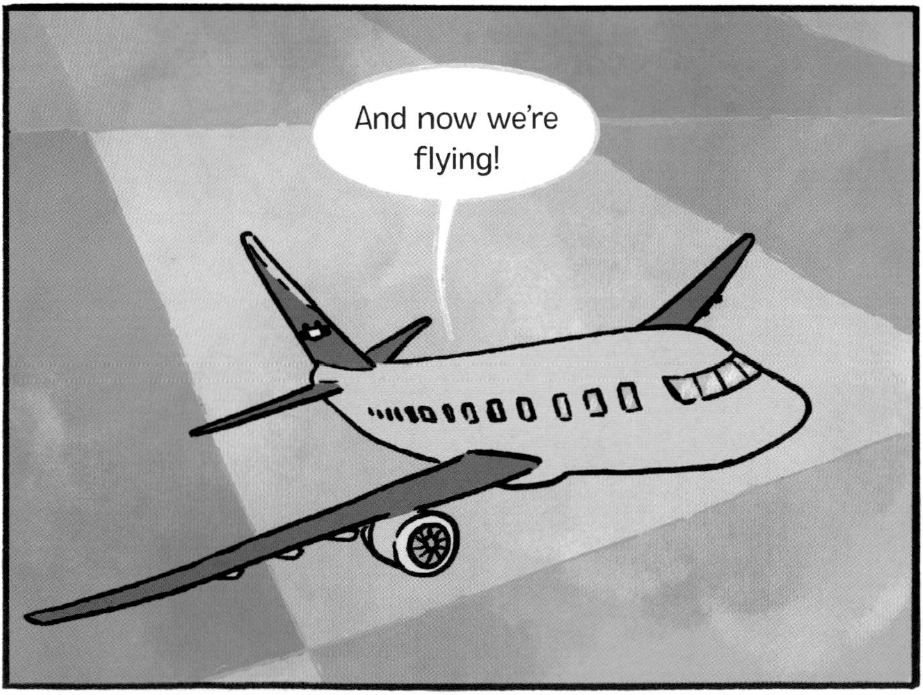
And now we're flying!

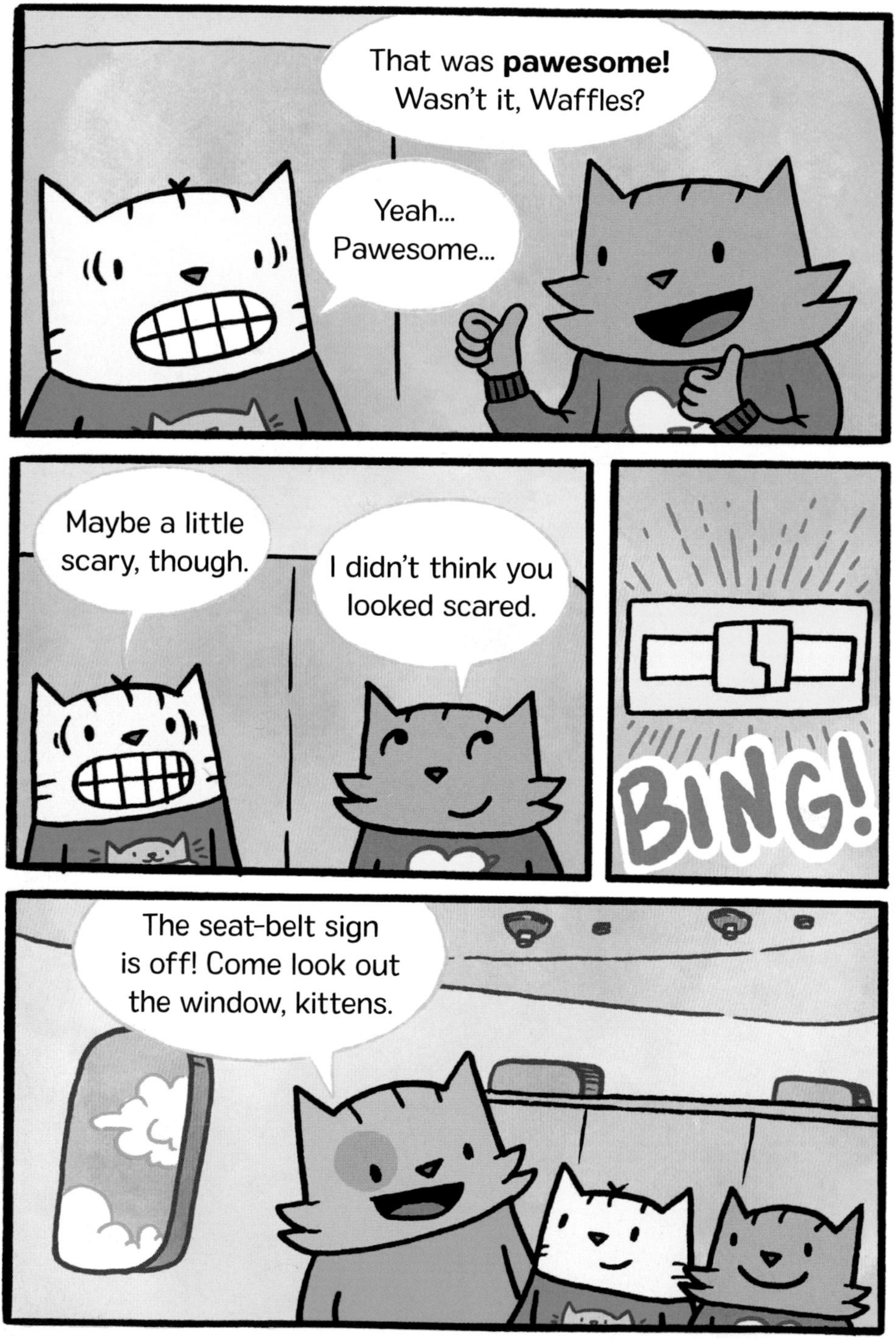
That was **pawesome!** Wasn't it, Waffles?
Yeah... Pawesome...
Maybe a little scary, though.
I didn't think you looked scared.
BING!
The seat-belt sign is off! Come look out the window, kittens.

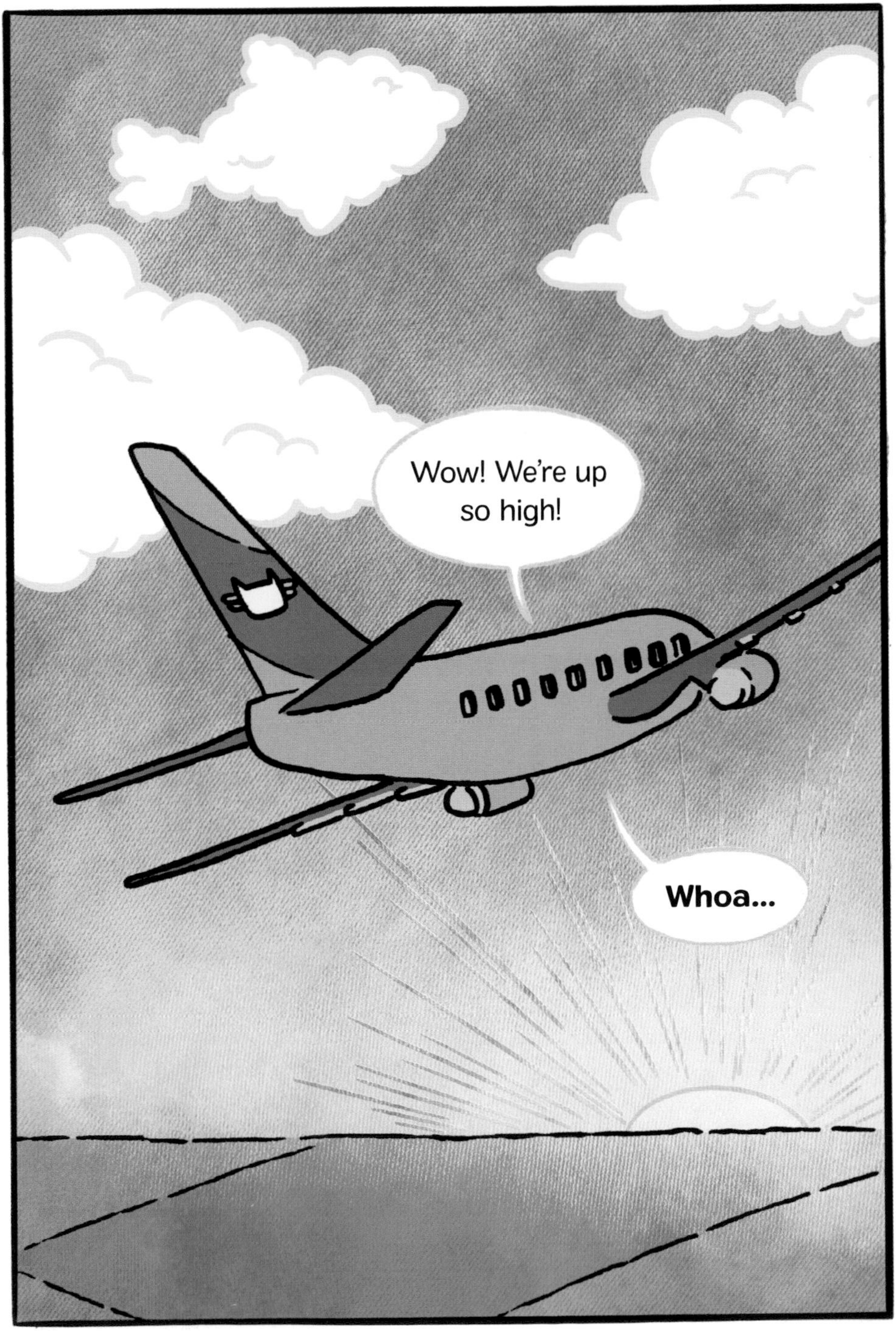
Wow! We're up so high!
Whoa...

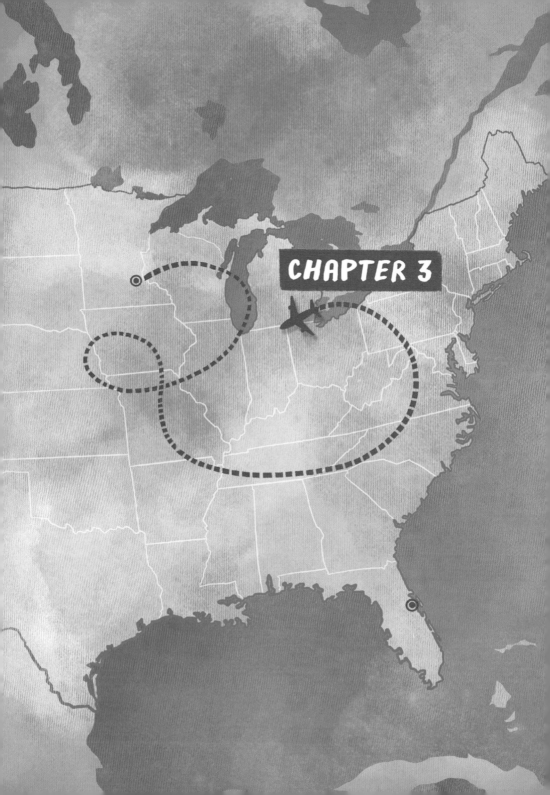

CHAPTER 3

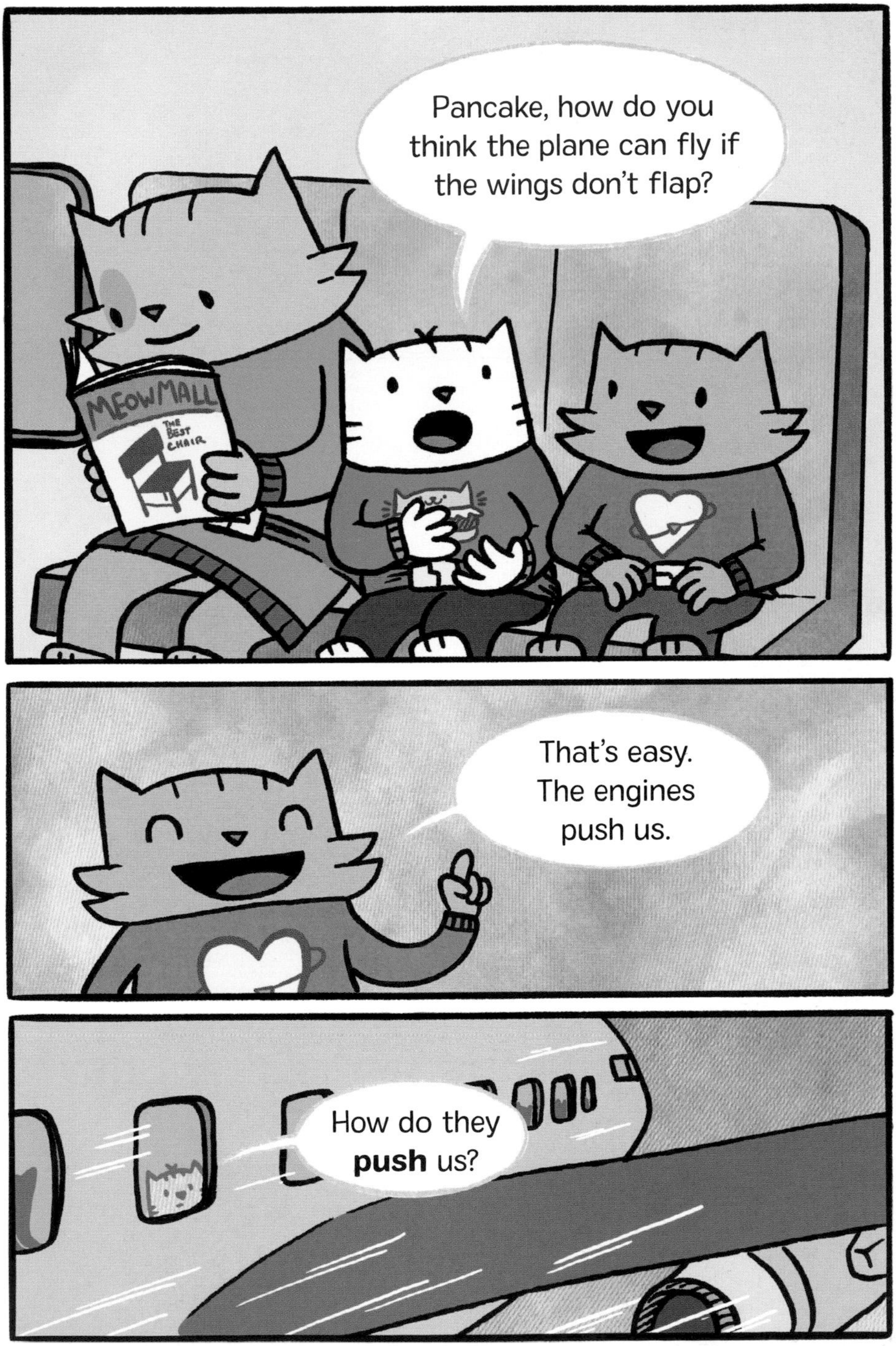

Pancake, how do you think the plane can fly if the wings don't flap?
MEOWMALL
THE BEST CHAIR
That's easy. The engines push us.
How do they **push** us?

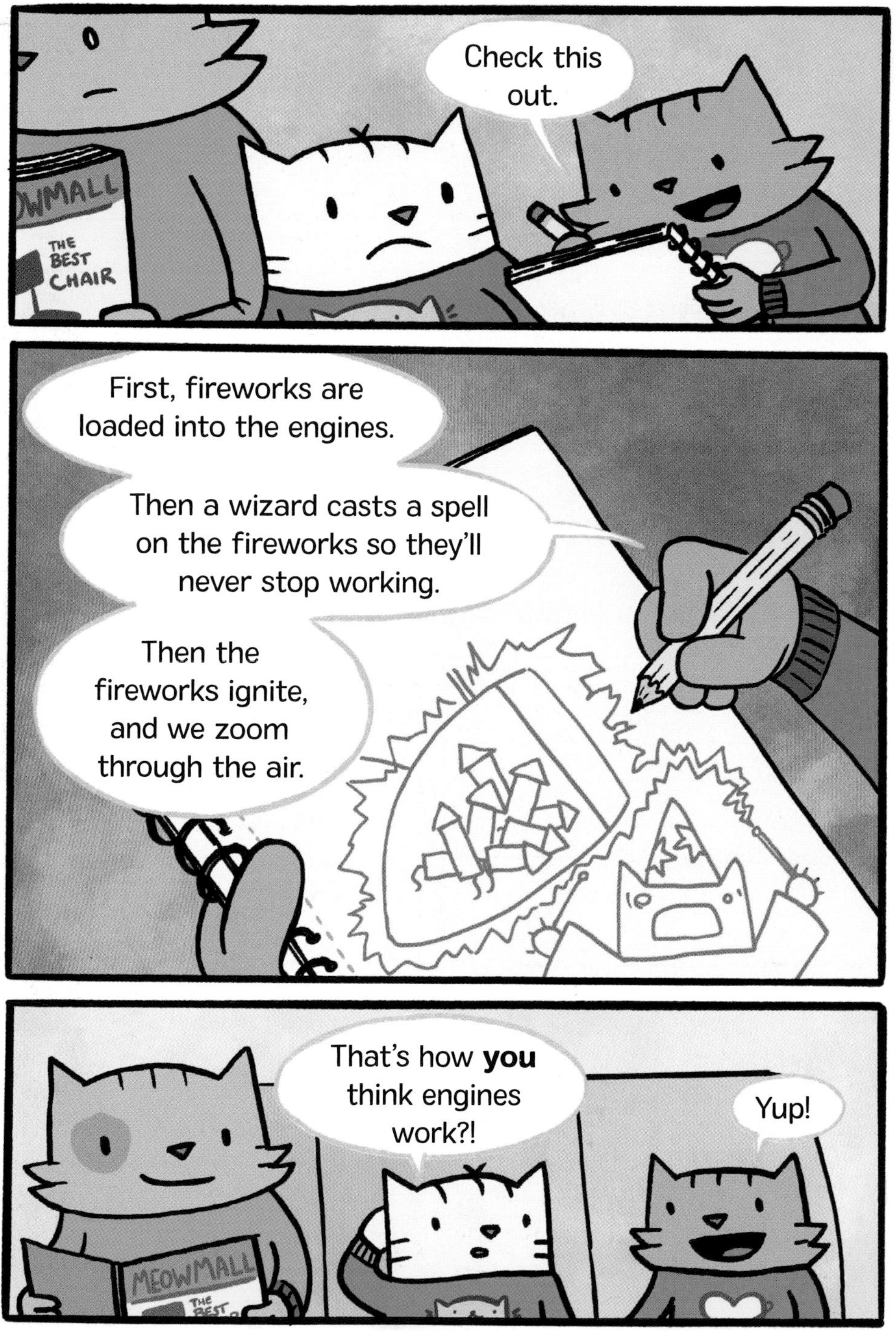
Check this out.
MEOWMALL
THE BEST CHAIR
First, fireworks are loaded into the engines.
Then a wizard casts a spell on the fireworks so they'll never stop working.
Then the fireworks ignite, and we zoom through the air.
That's how **you** think engines work?!
Yup!
MEOWMALL
THE BEST

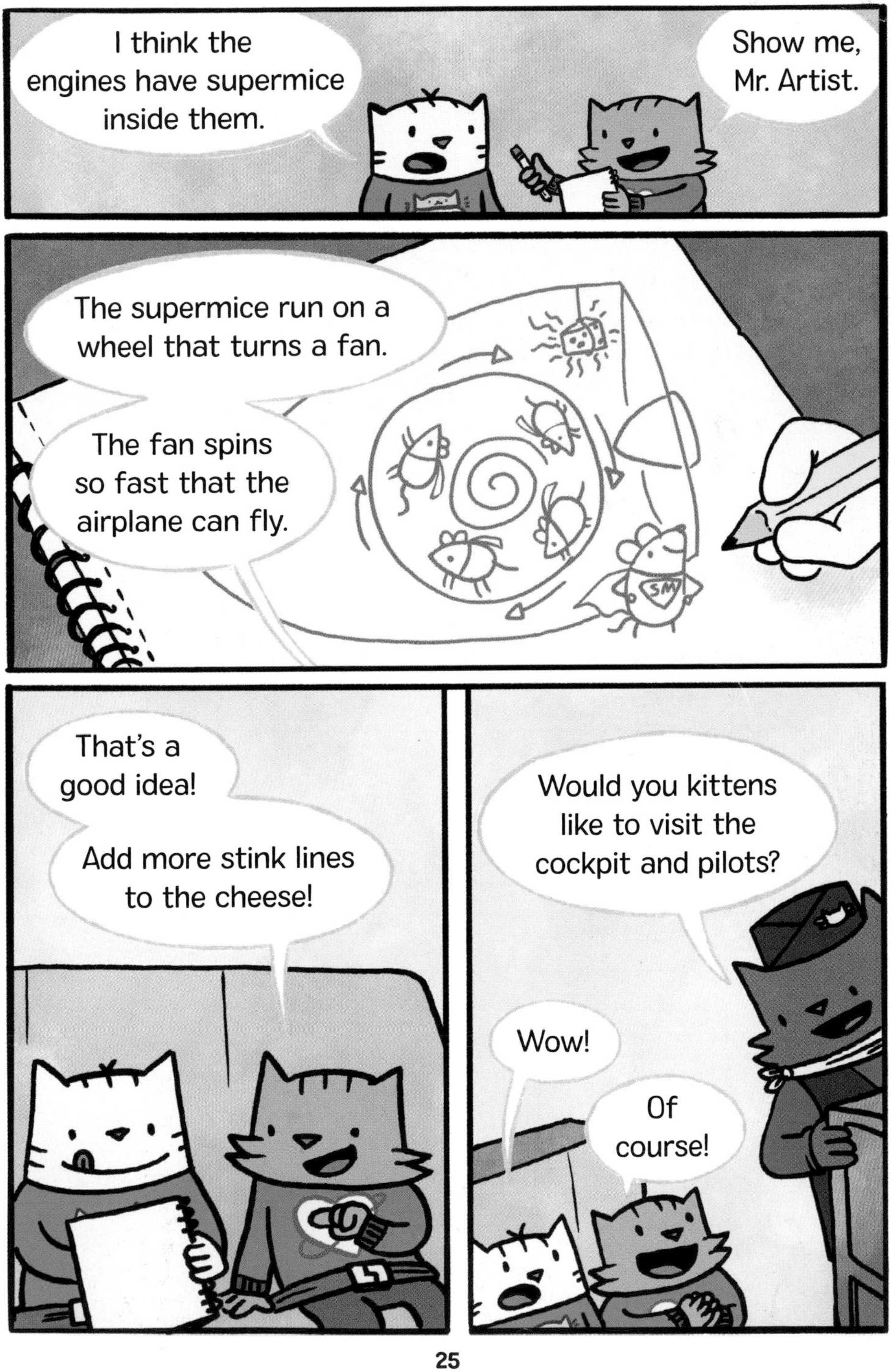
I think the engines have supermice inside them.
Show me, Mr. Artist.
The supermice run on a wheel that turns a fan.
The fan spins so fast that the airplane can fly.
SM
That's a good idea!
Add more stink lines to the cheese!
Would you kittens like to visit the cockpit and pilots?
Wow!
Of course!

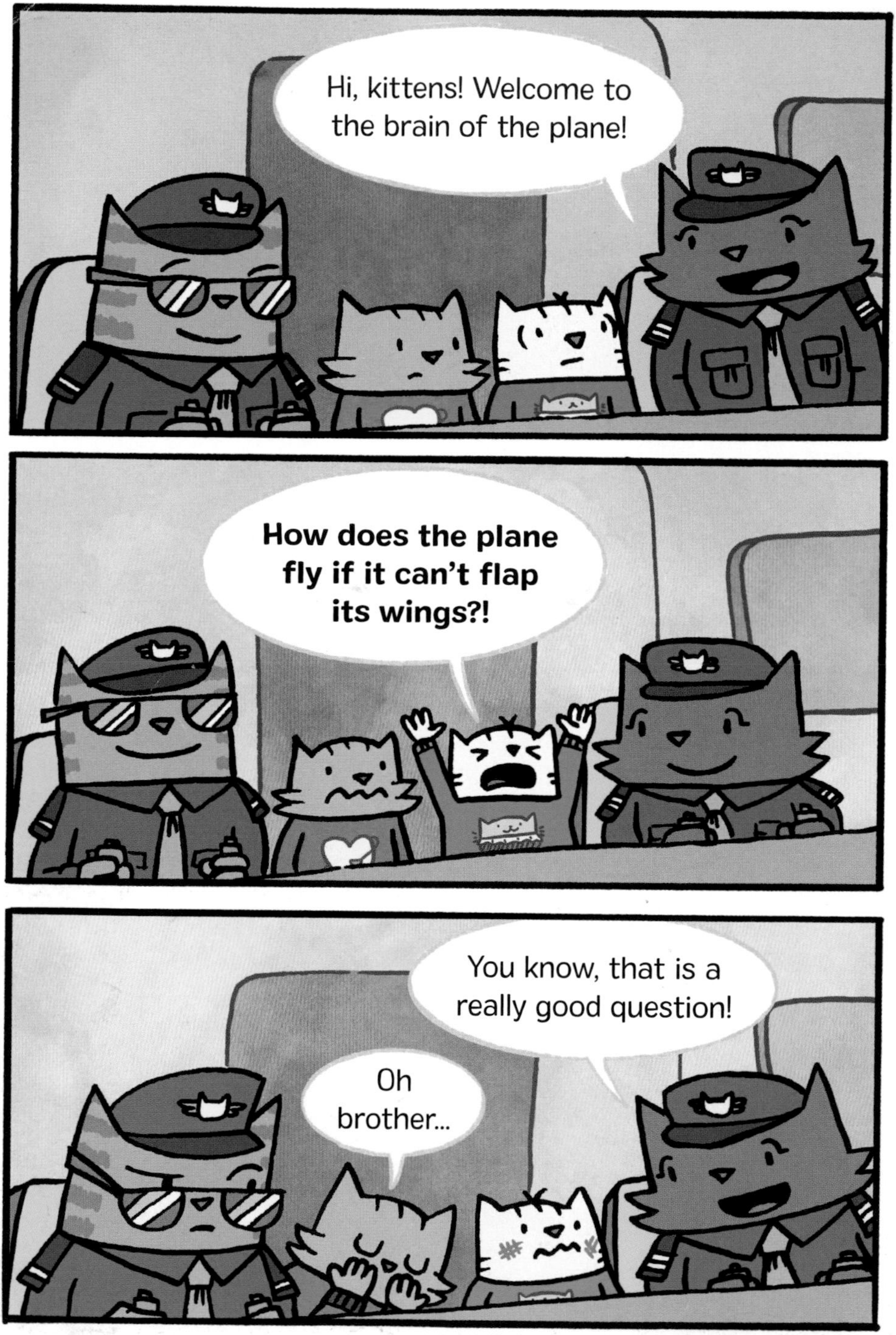

Hi, kittens! Welcome to the brain of the plane!
How does the plane fly if it can't flap its wings?!
You know, that is a really good question!
Oh brother...

Airplane wings are kind of like bird wings.
They are both flat on the bottom and curved on the top.
When air flows over the wings, it takes longer to go over the curved tops than it does to go under the flat bottoms.
The wings are held up by the air underneath, and that lifts the plane into the sky.

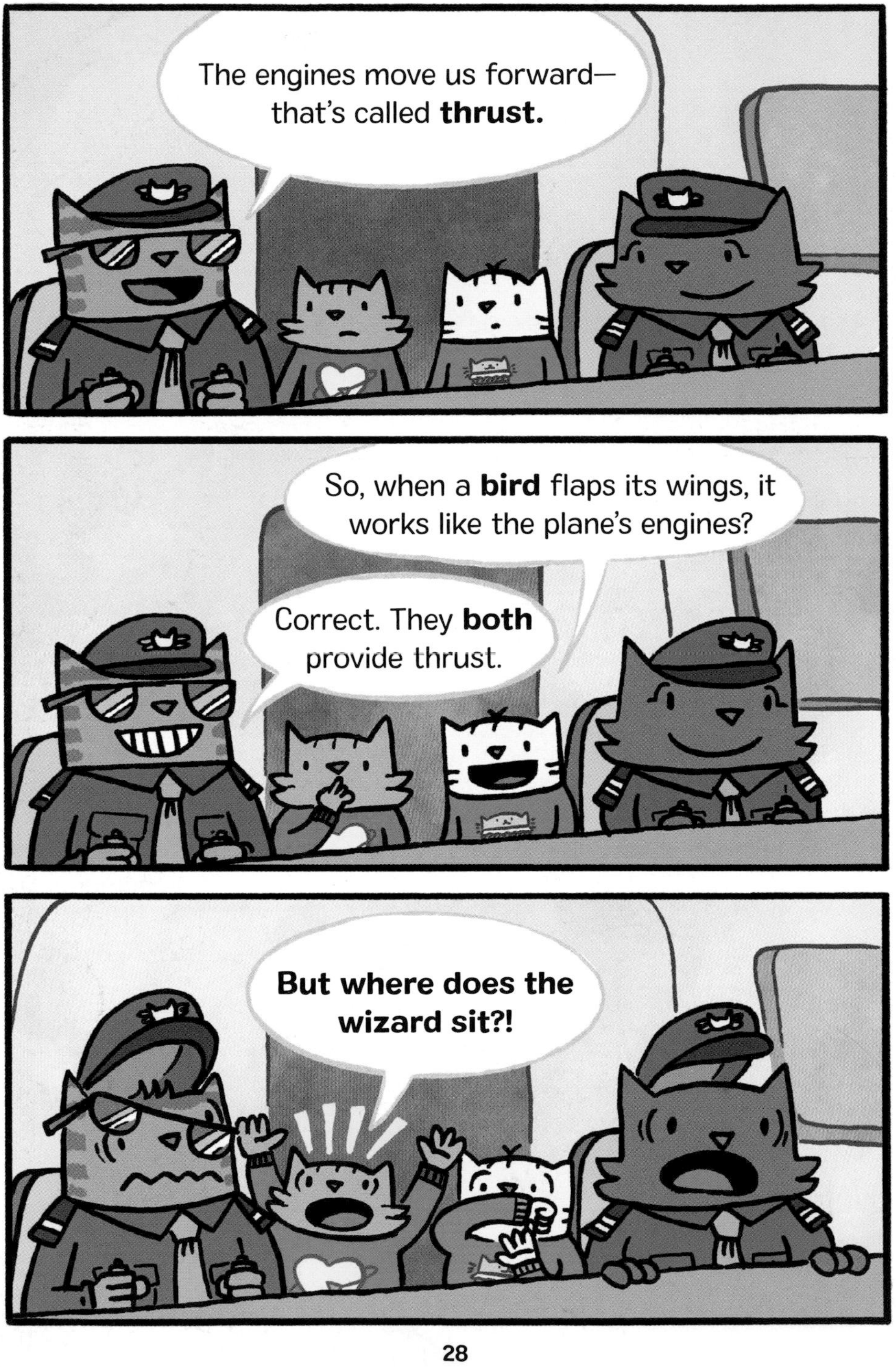
The engines move us forward—that's called **thrust.**
So, when a **bird** flaps its wings, it works like the plane's engines?
Correct. They **both** provide thrust.
But where does the wizard sit?!

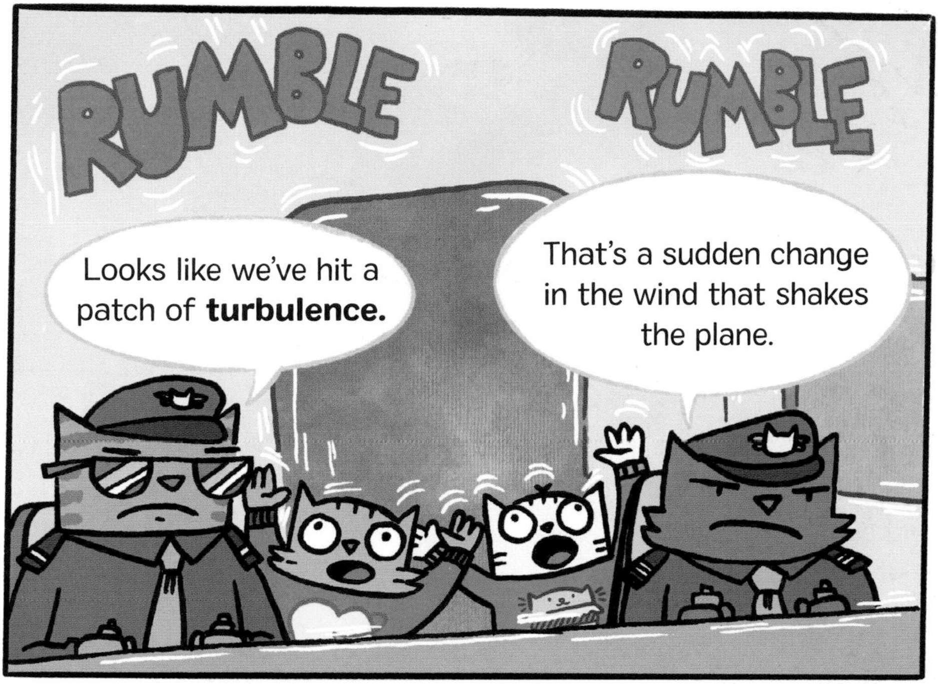
RUMBLE
RUMBLE
Looks like we've hit a patch of **turbulence.**
That's a sudden change in the wind that shakes the plane.

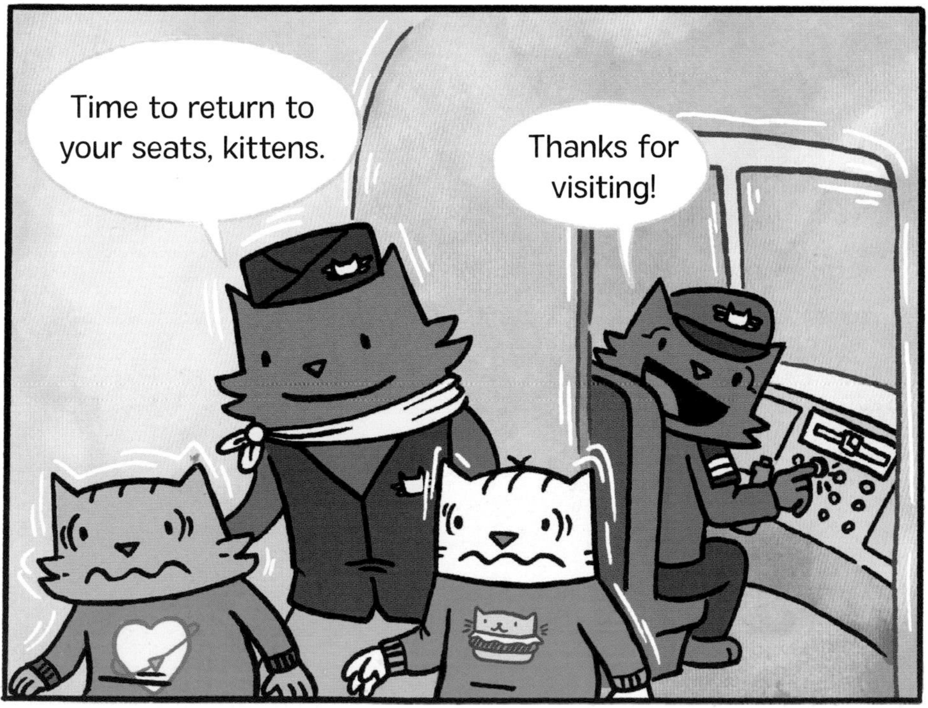
Time to return to your seats, kittens.
Thanks for visiting!

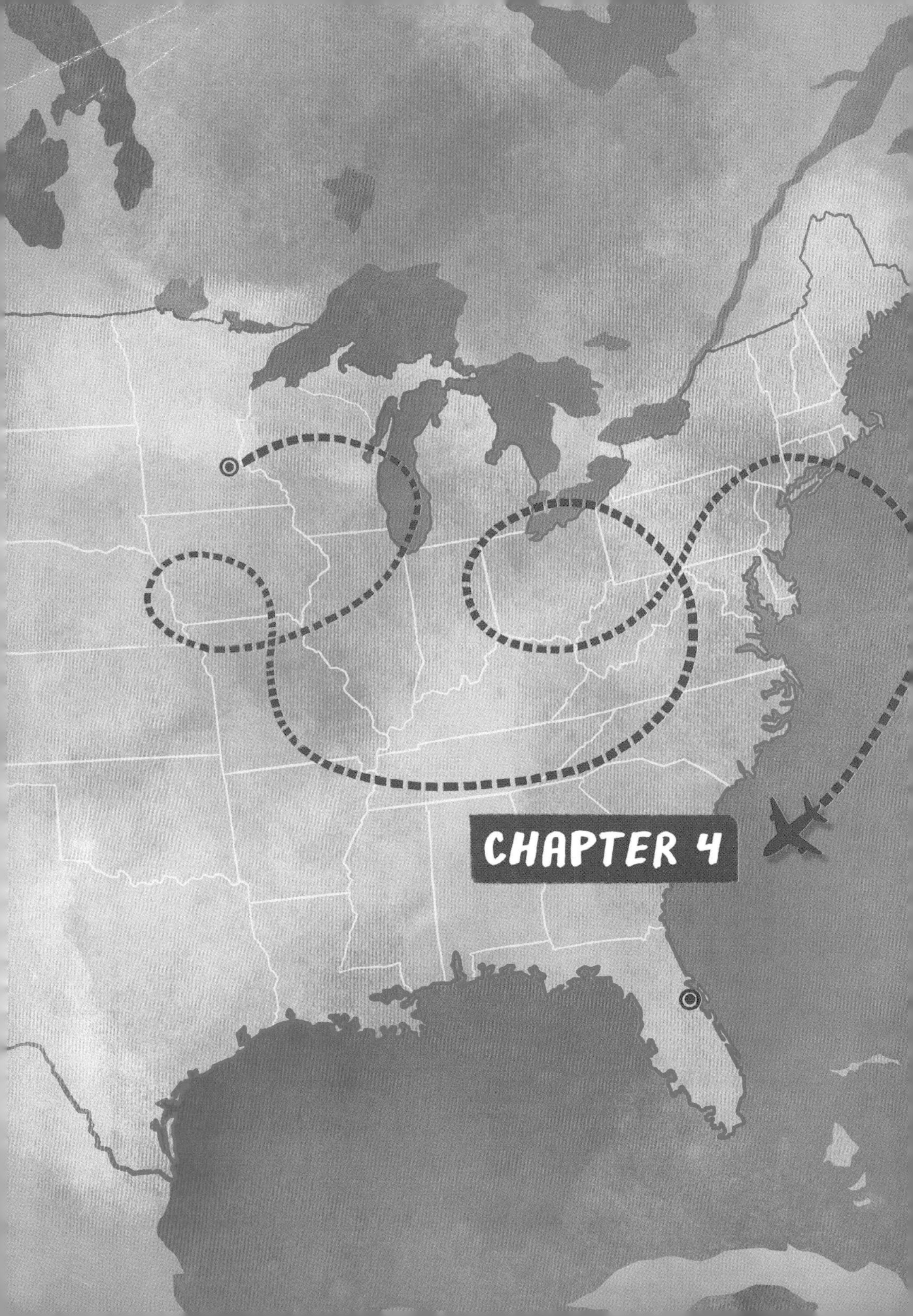
CHAPTER 4

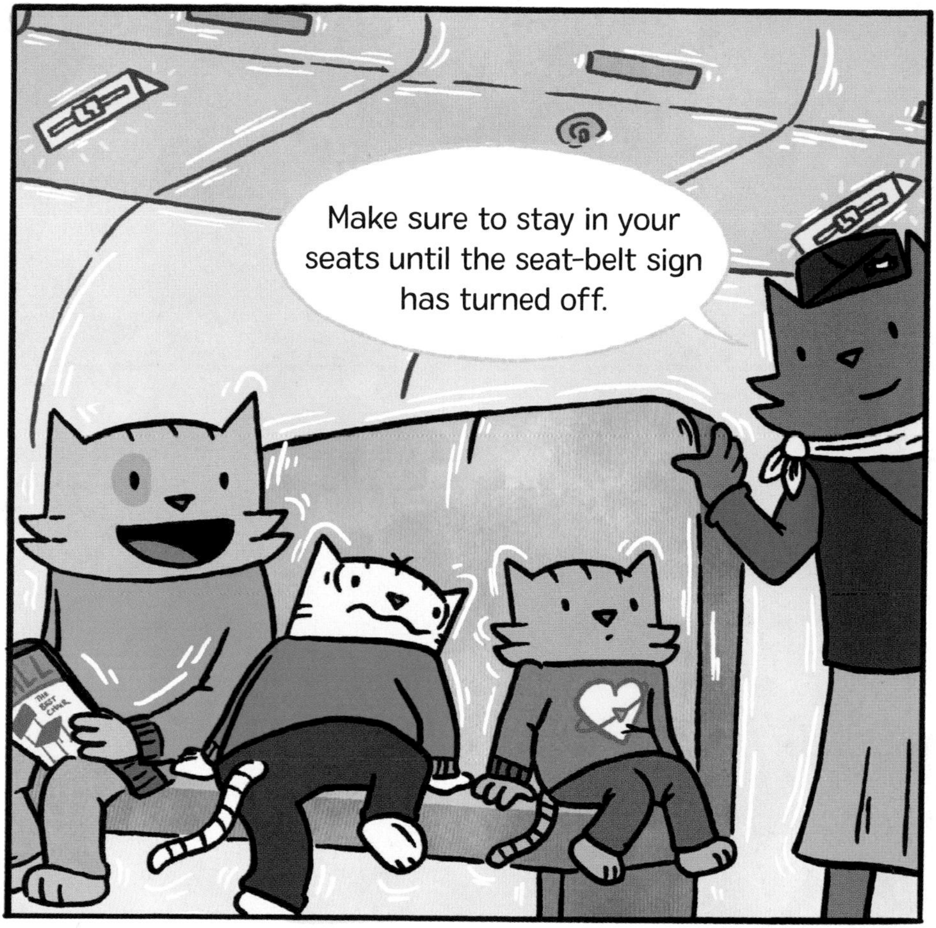
Make sure to stay in your seats until the seat-belt sign has turned off.

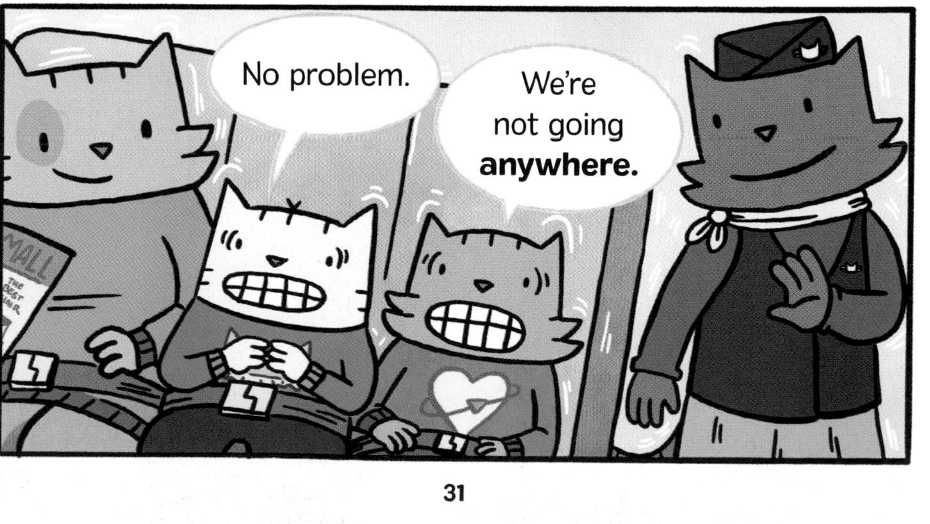
No problem.
We're not going **anywhere.**

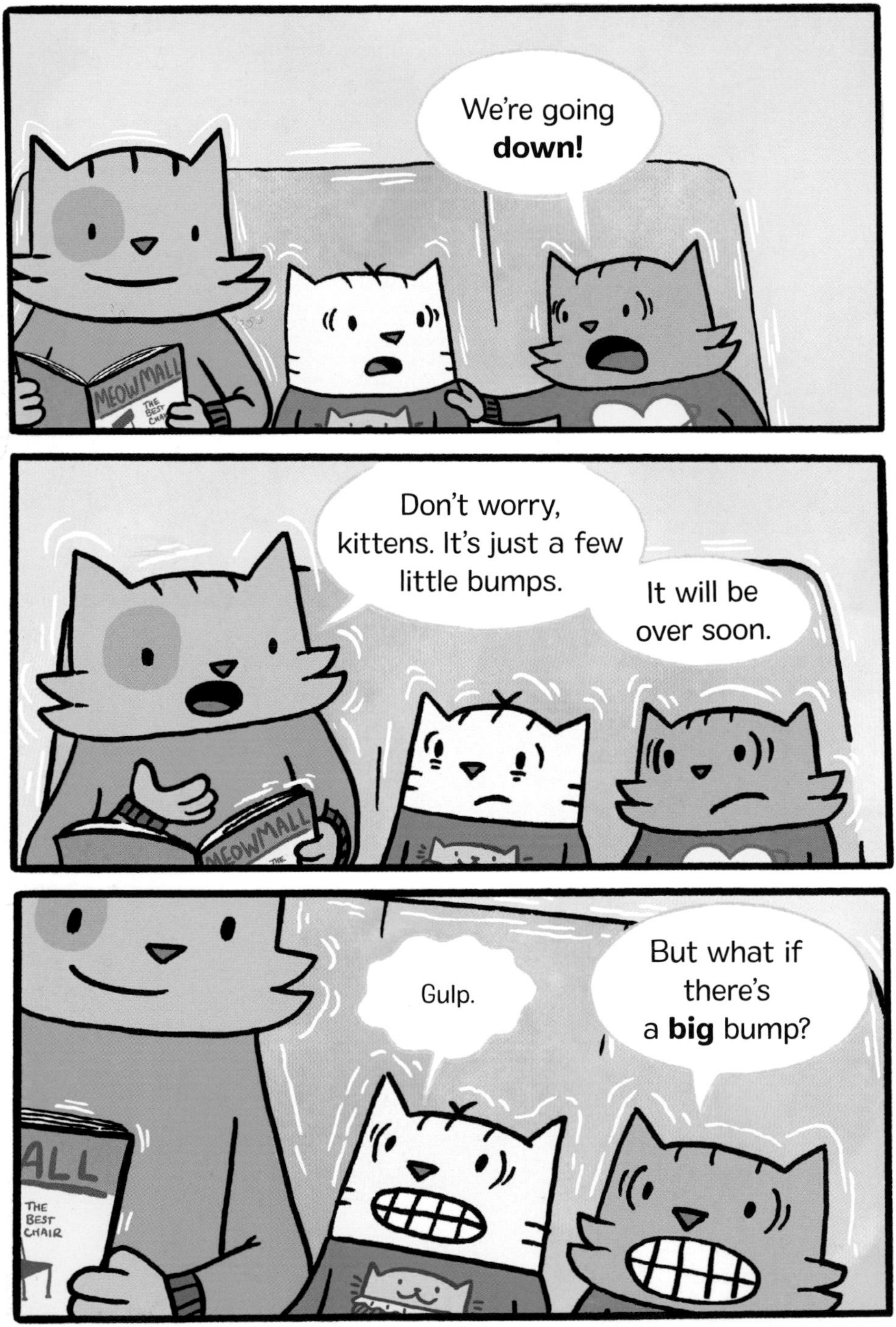
We're going **down!**
MEOWMALL
THE BEST CHAIR
Don't worry, kittens. It's just a few little bumps.
It will be over soon.
MEOWMALL
Gulp.
But what if there's a **big** bump?
ALL
THE BEST CHAIR

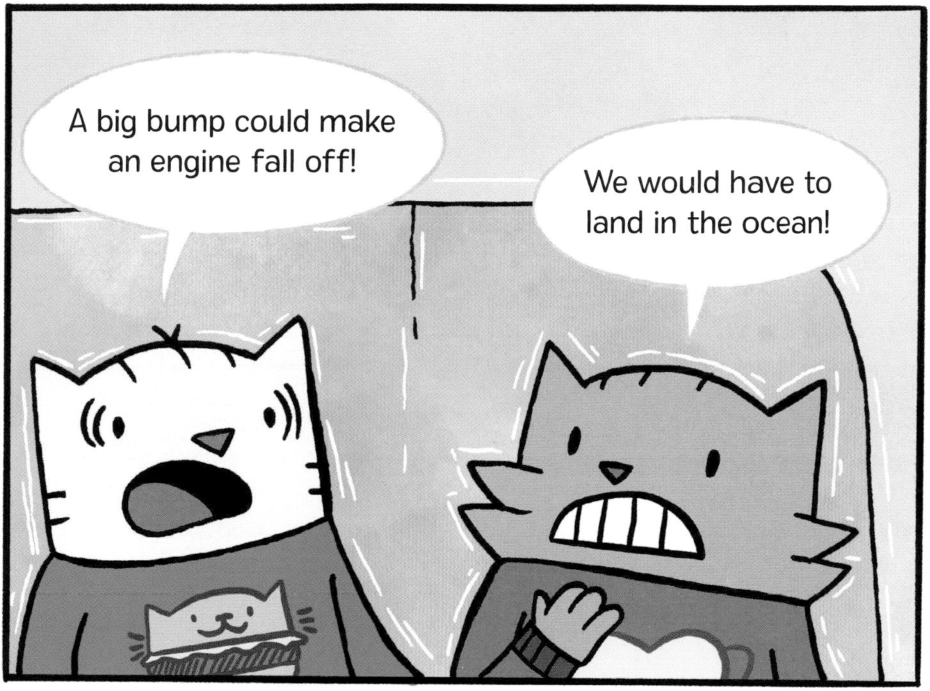
A big bump could make an engine fall off!
We would have to land in the ocean!

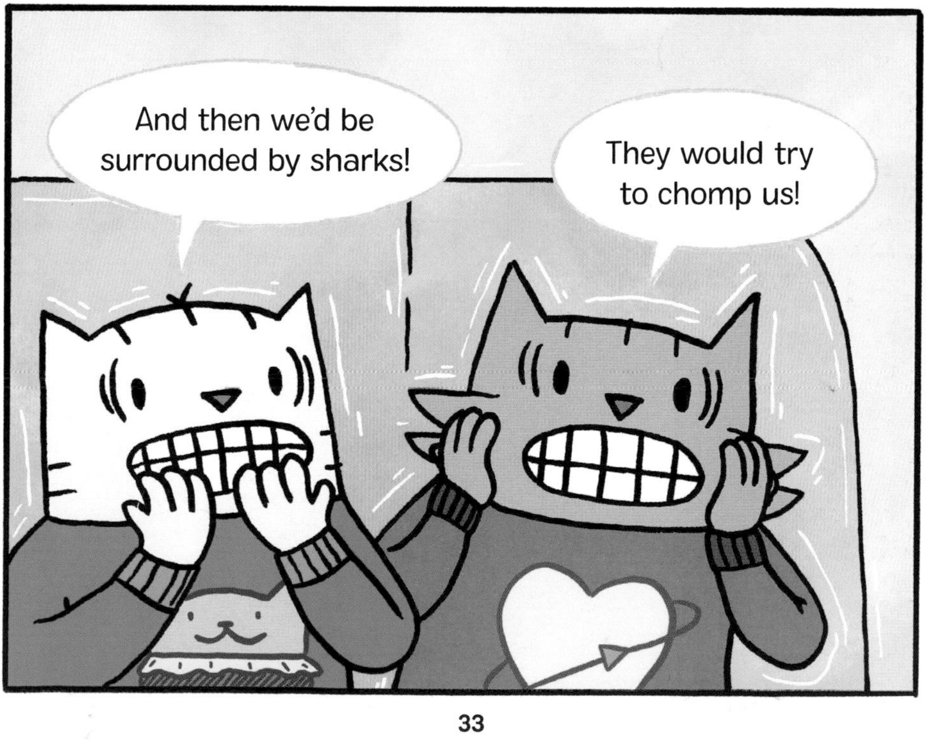
And then we'd be surrounded by sharks!
They would try to chomp us!

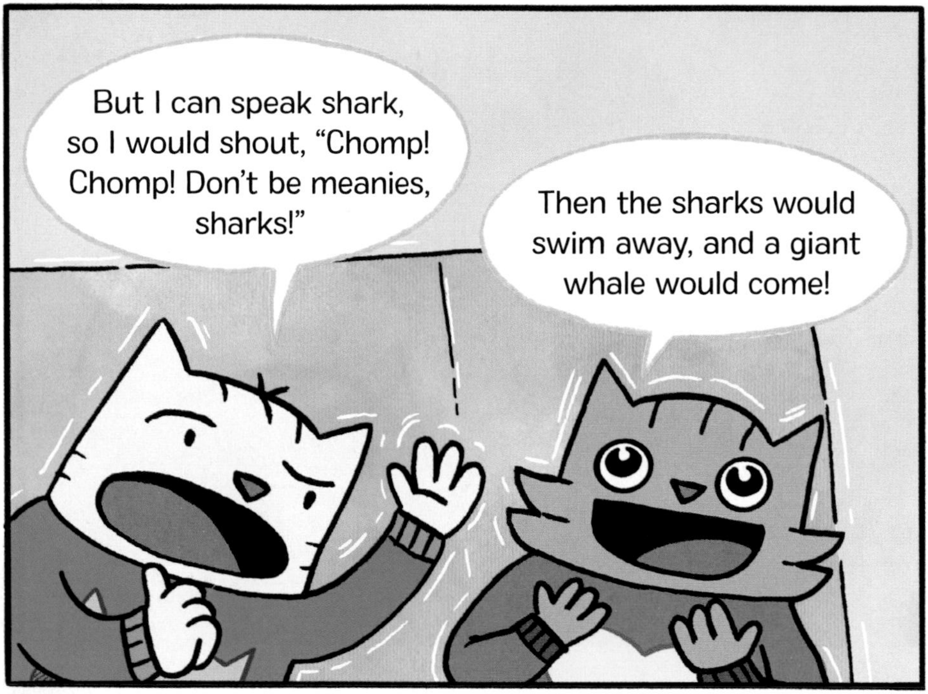
But I can speak shark, so I would shout, "Chomp! Chomp! Don't be meanies, sharks!"
Then the sharks would swim away, and a giant whale would come!

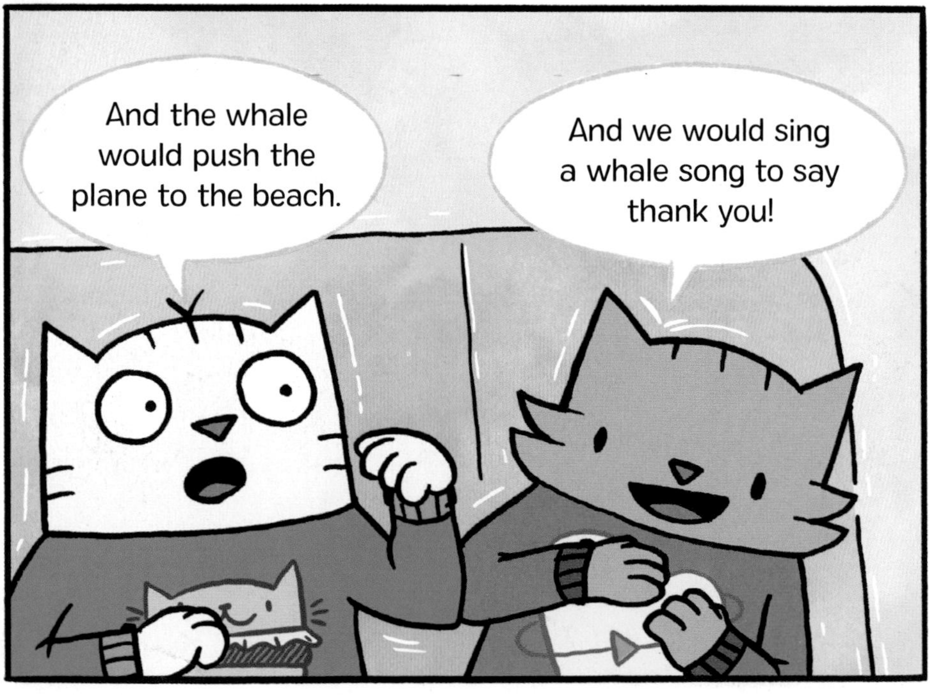
And the whale would push the plane to the beach.
And we would sing a whale song to say thank you!

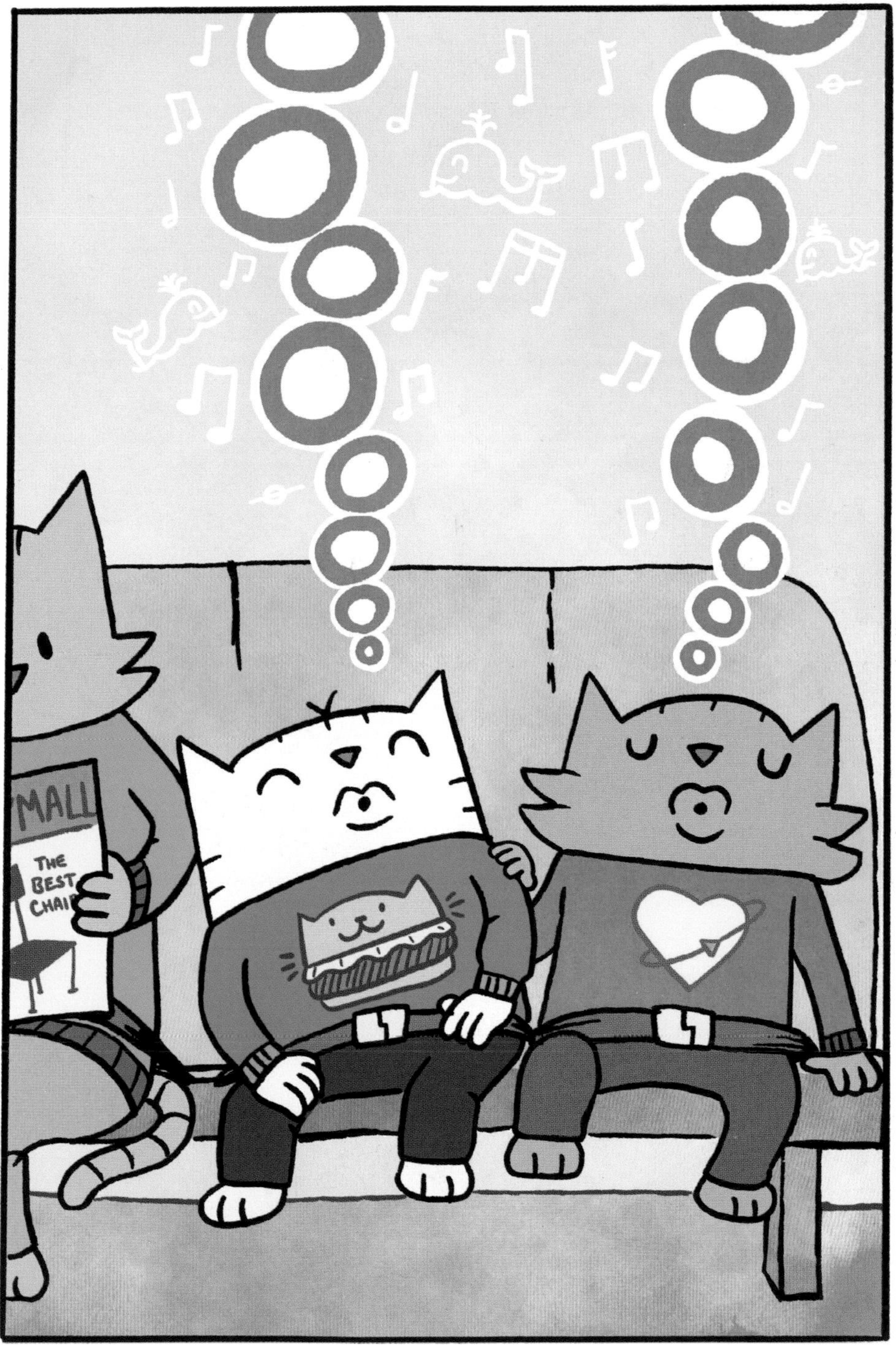
MALL
THE
BEST
CHAI

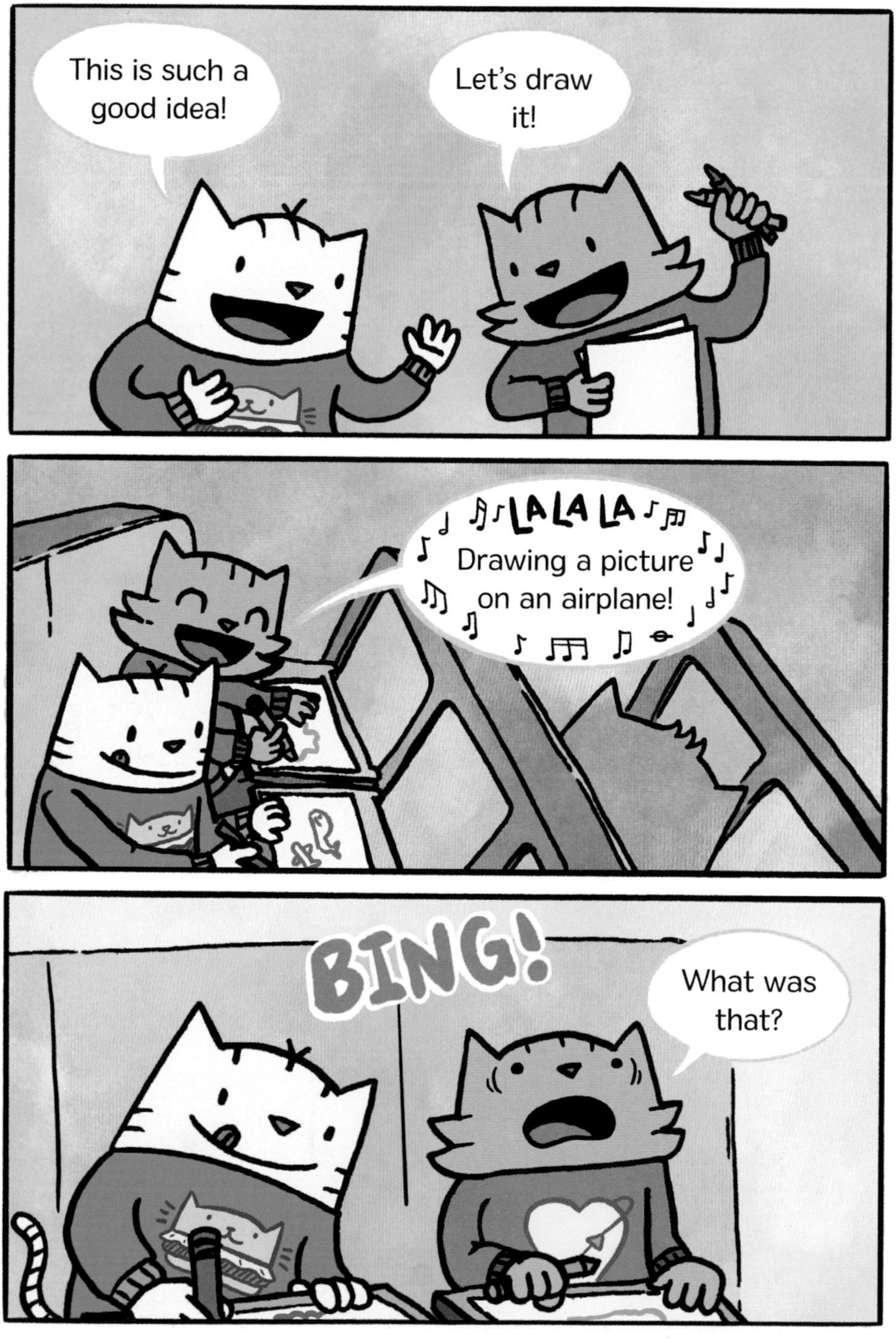
This is such a good idea!
Let's draw it!
LA LA LA
Drawing a picture on an airplane!
BING!
What was that?

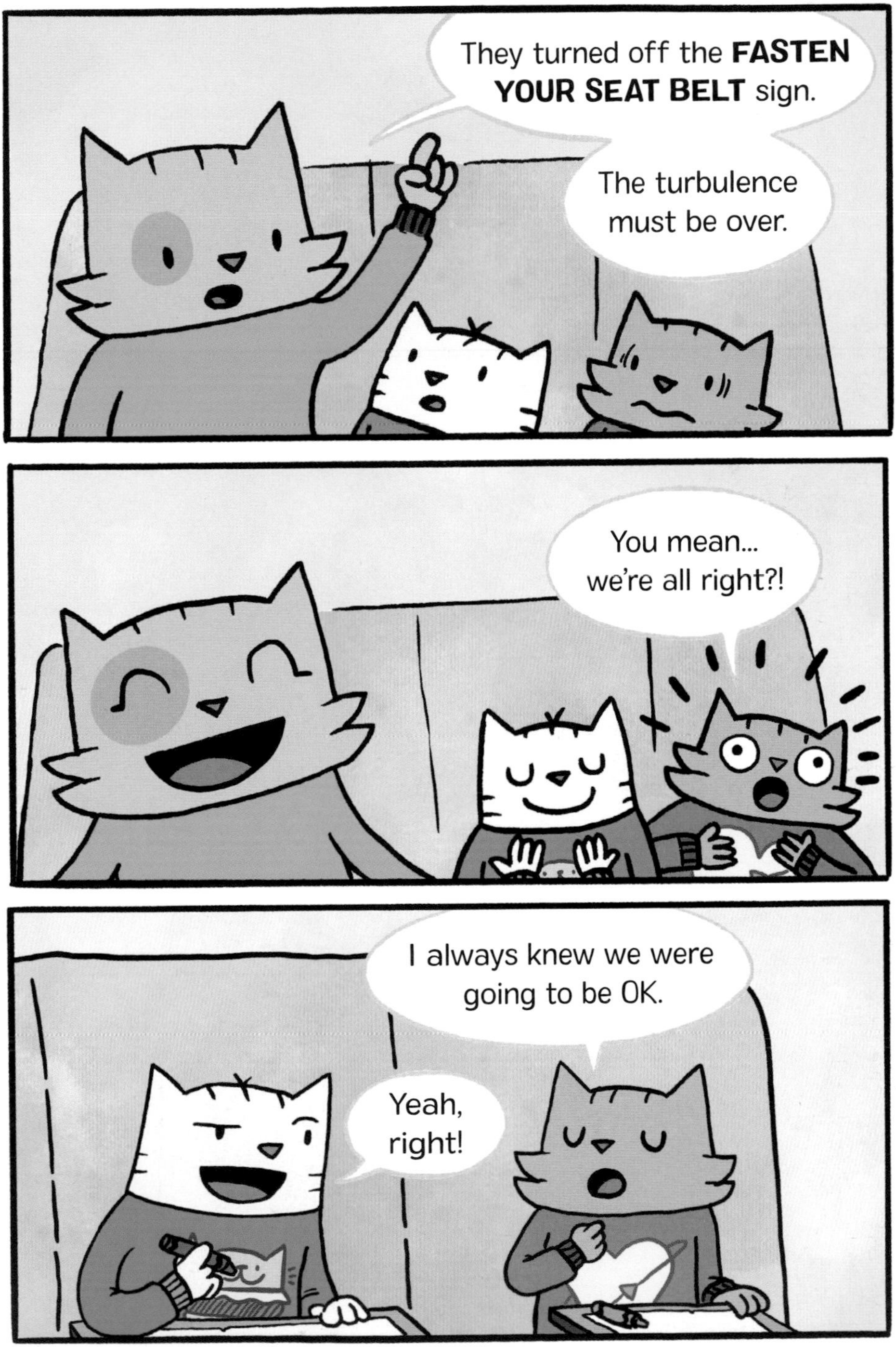
They turned off the **FASTEN YOUR SEAT BELT** sign.
The turbulence must be over.
You mean... we're all right?!
I always knew we were going to be OK.
Yeah, right!

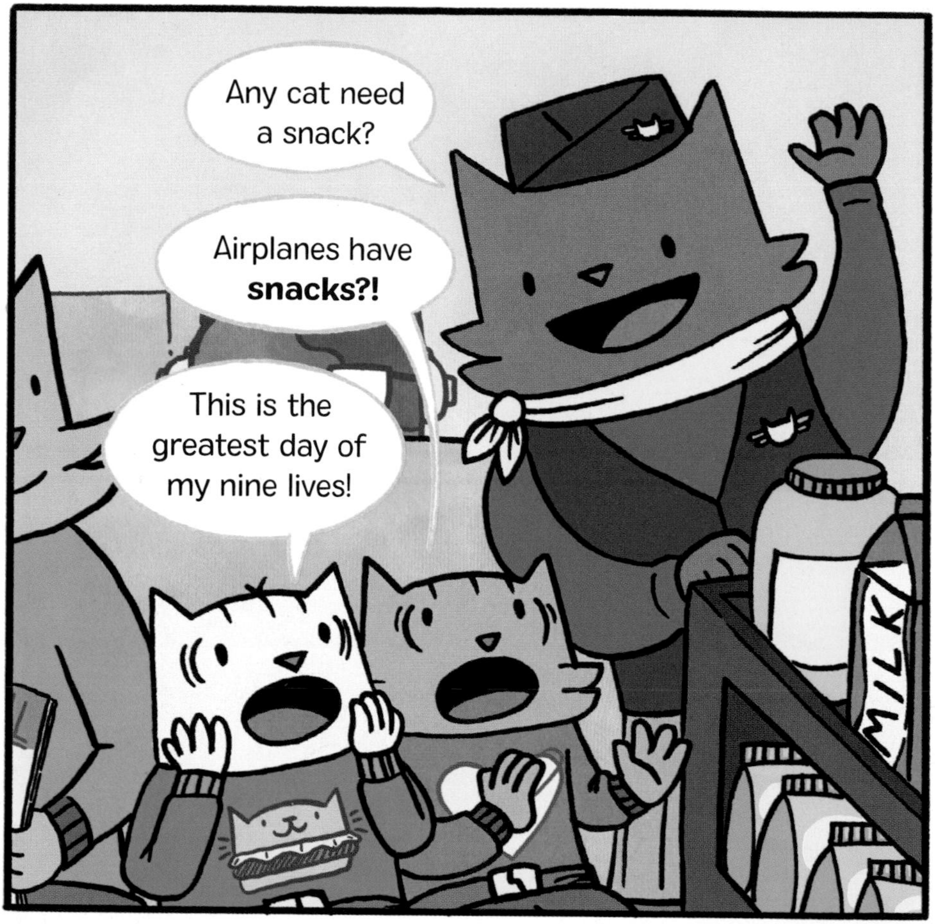
Any cat need a snack?
Airplanes have **snacks?!**
This is the greatest day of my nine lives!
MILK

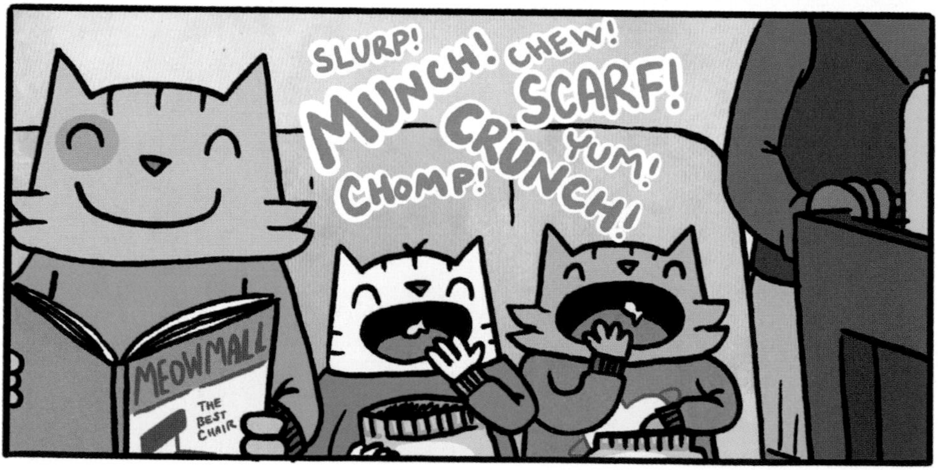
SLURP!
MUNCH!
CHEW!
SCARF!
CRUNCH!
YUM!
CHOMP!
MEOWMALL
THE BEST CHAIR

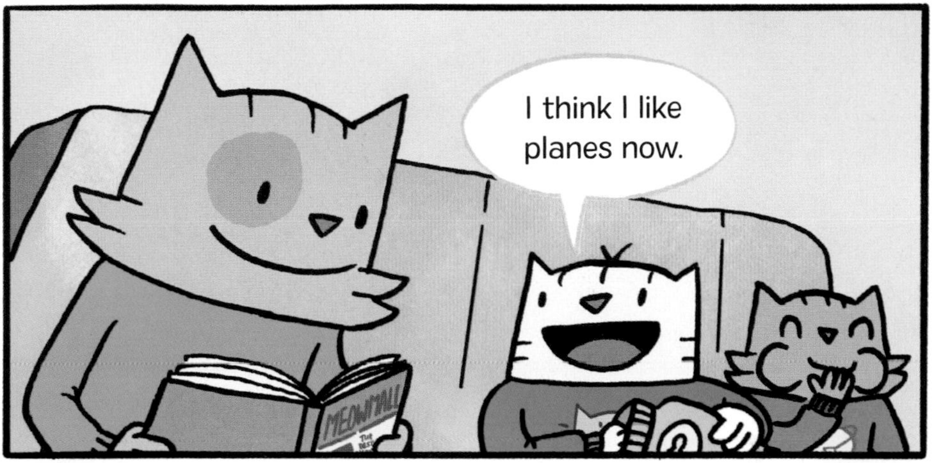
I think I like planes now.

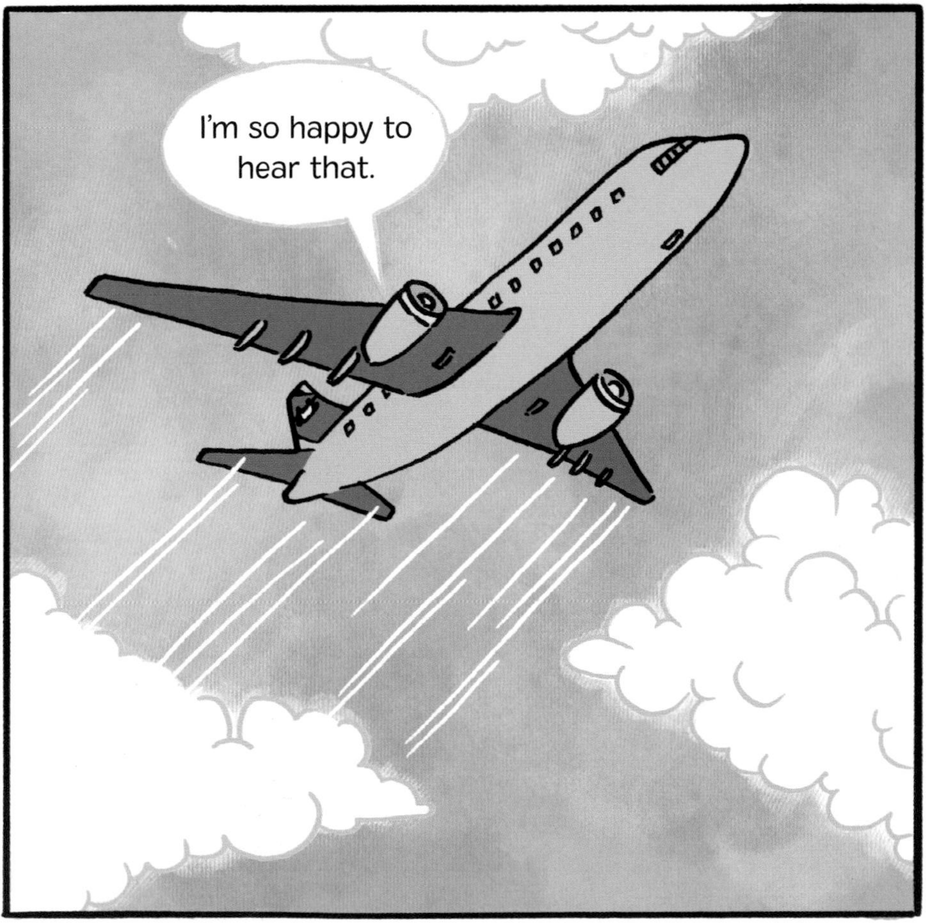
I'm so happy to hear that.

CHAPTER 5

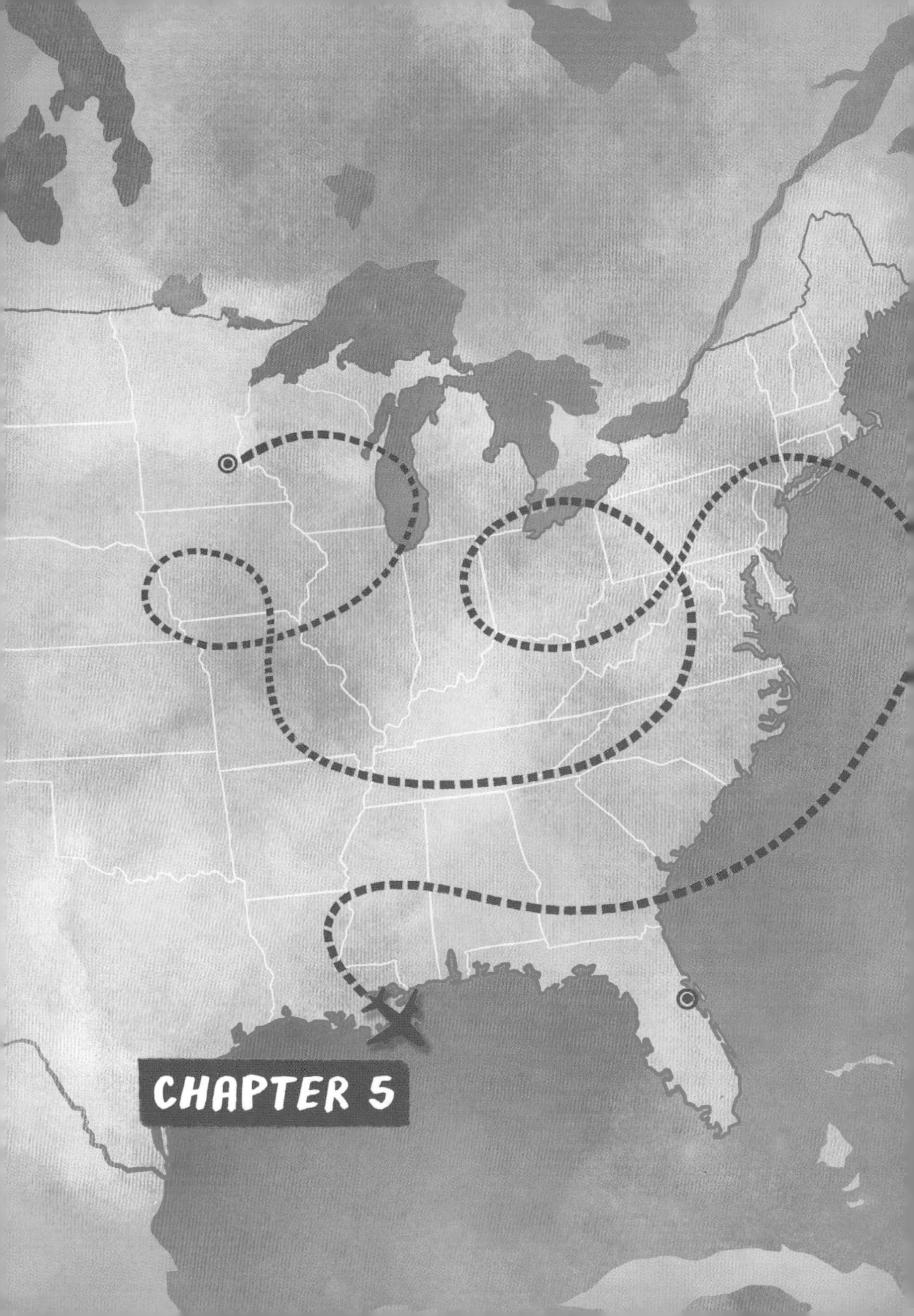

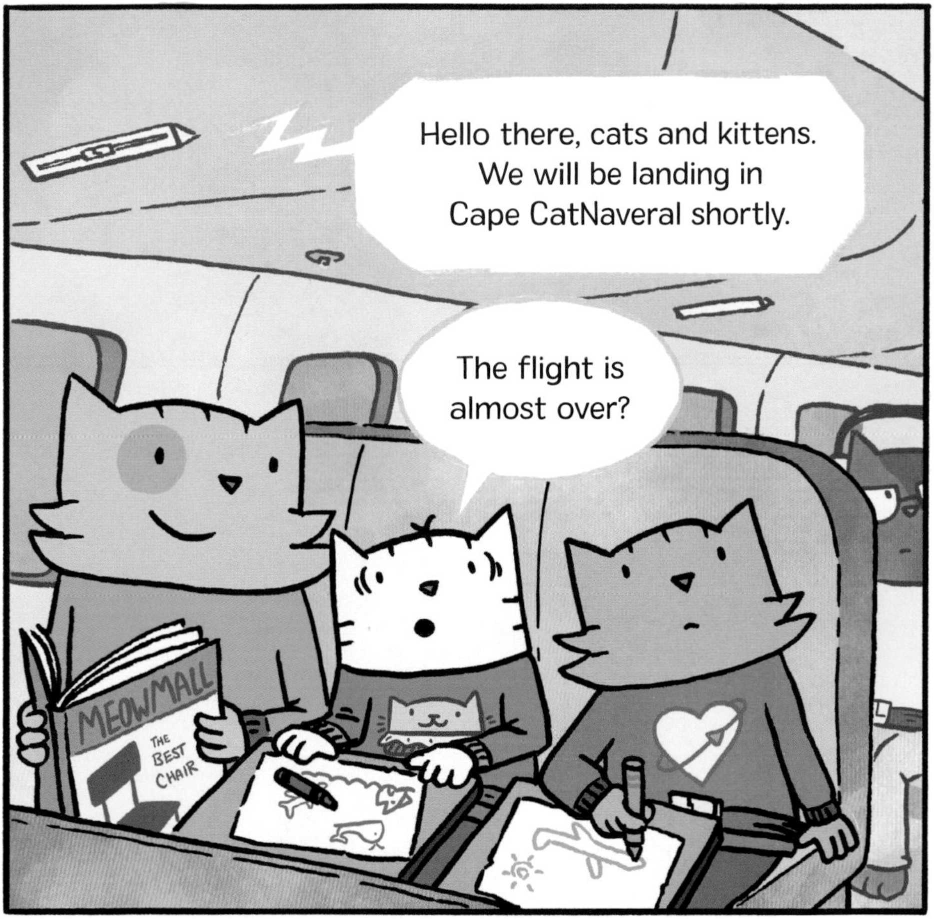
Hello there, cats and kittens. We will be landing in Cape CatNaveral shortly.
The flight is almost over?
MEOWMALL
THE BEST CHAIR

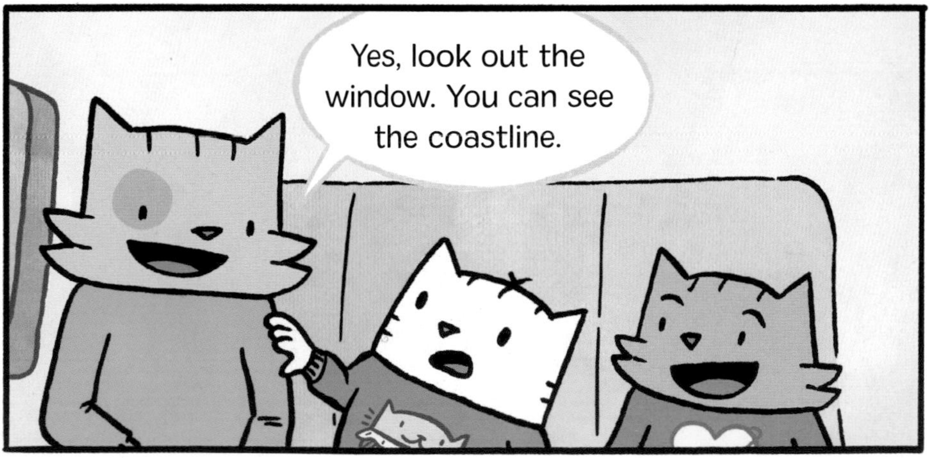
Yes, look out the window. You can see the coastline.

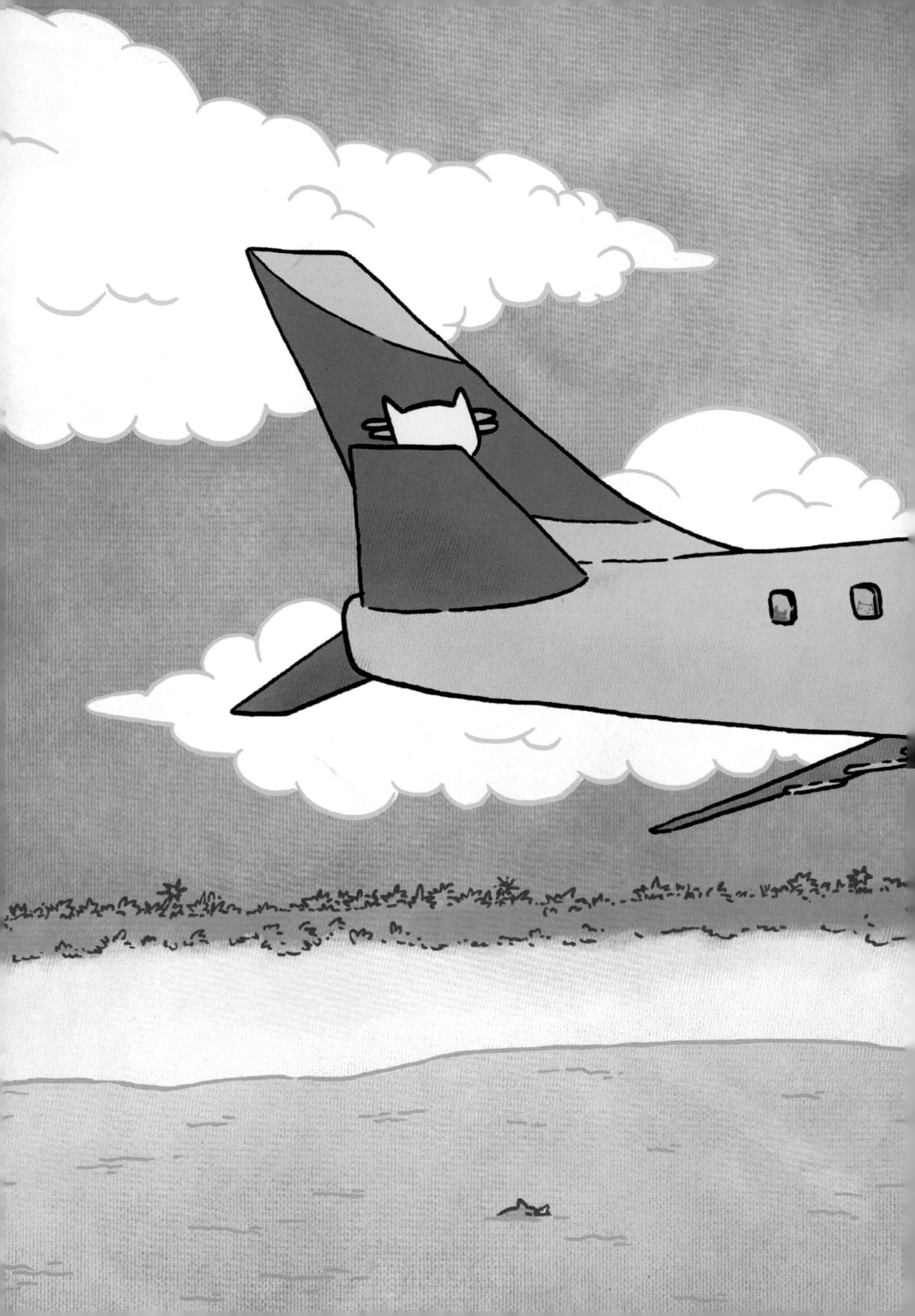

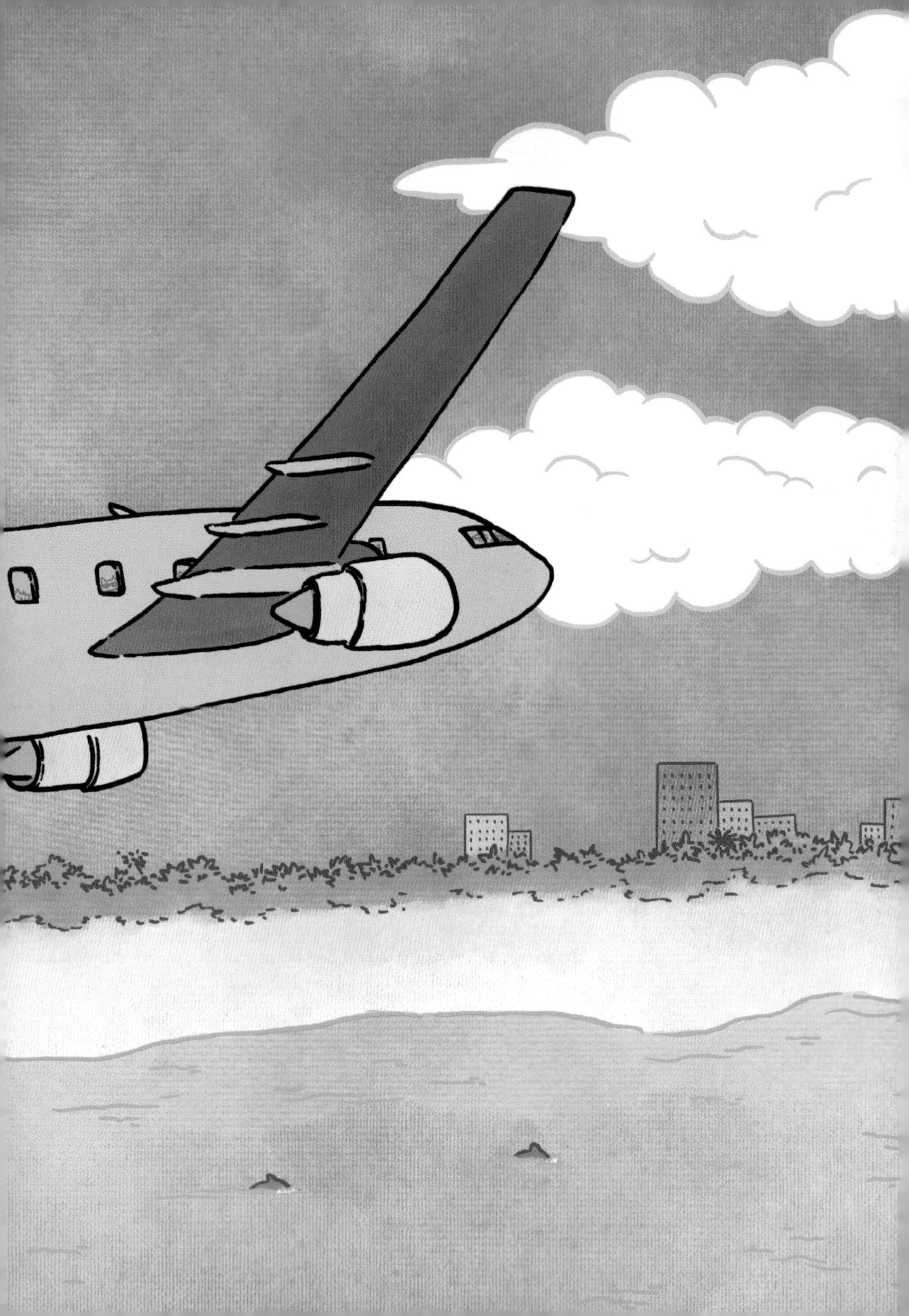

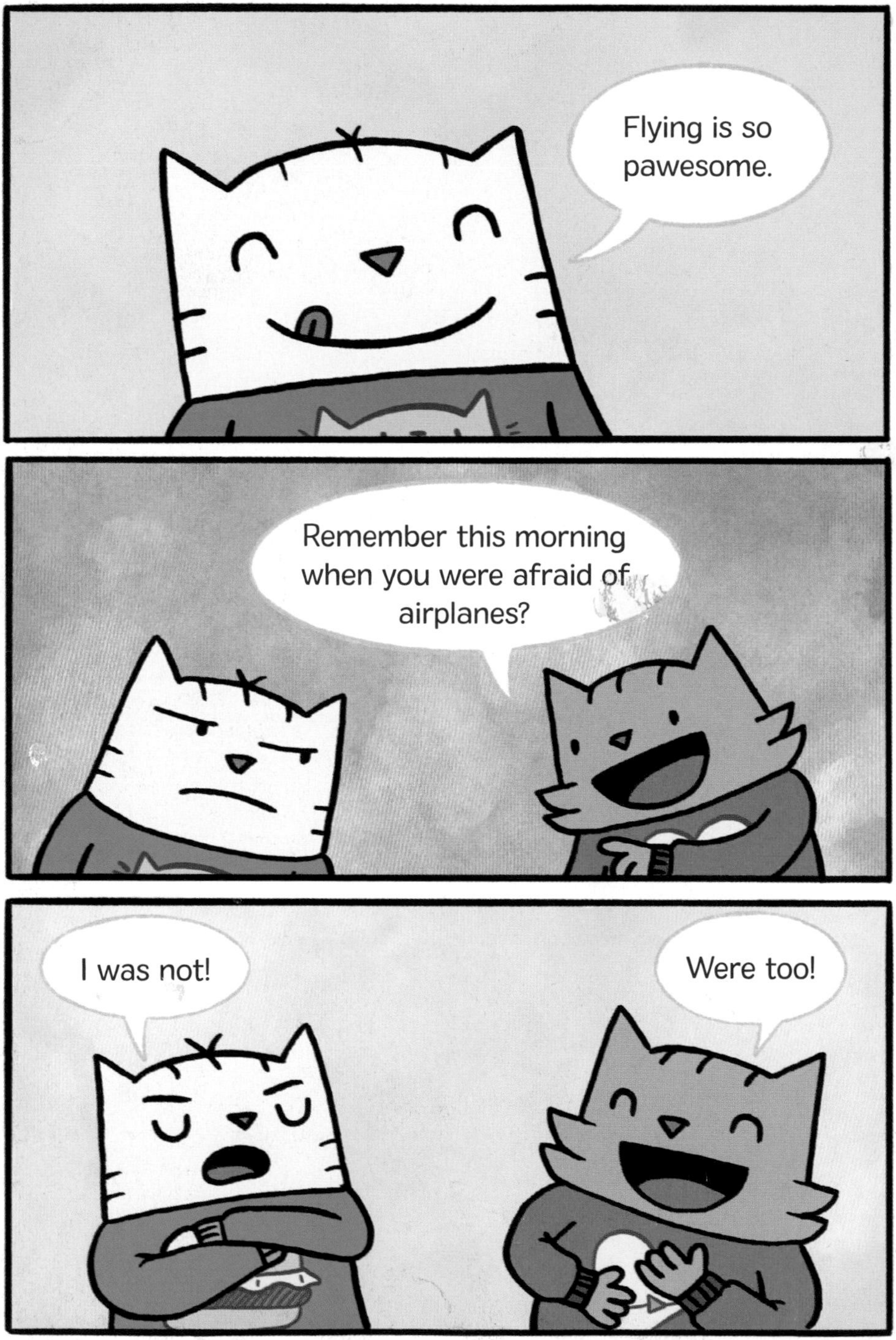

Flying is so pawesome.
Remember this morning when you were afraid of airplanes?
I was not!
Were too!

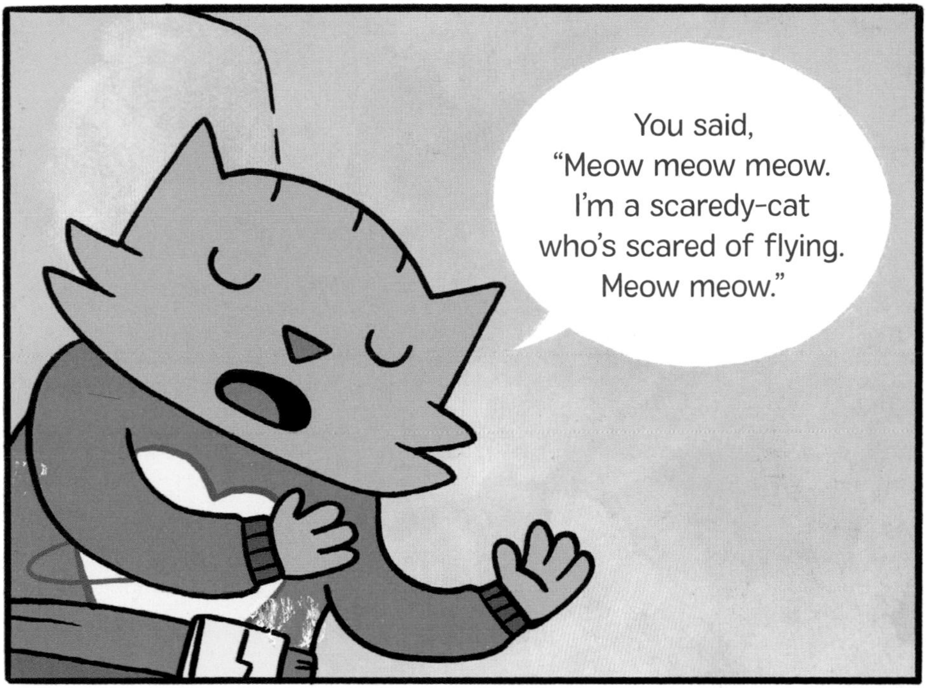
You said, "Meow meow meow. I'm a scaredy-cat who's scared of flying. Meow meow."

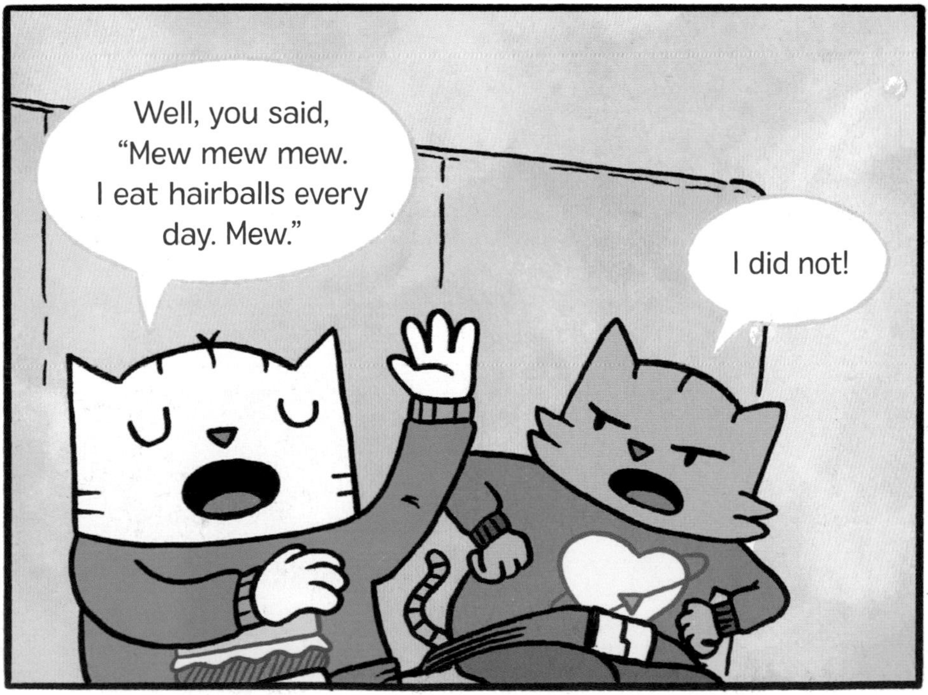
Well, you said, "Mew mew mew. I eat hairballs every day. Mew."
I did not!

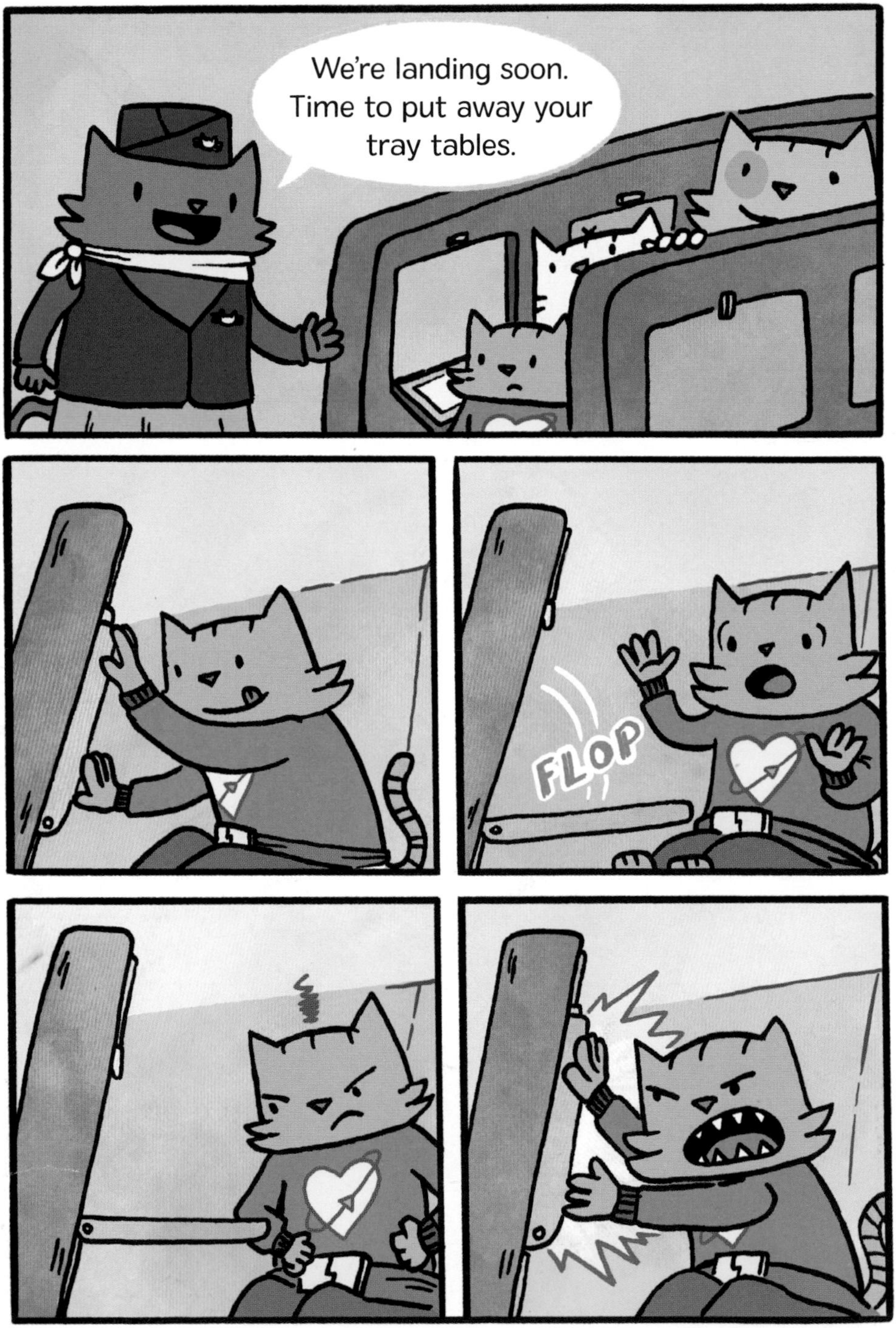
We're landing soon. Time to put away your tray tables.
FLOP

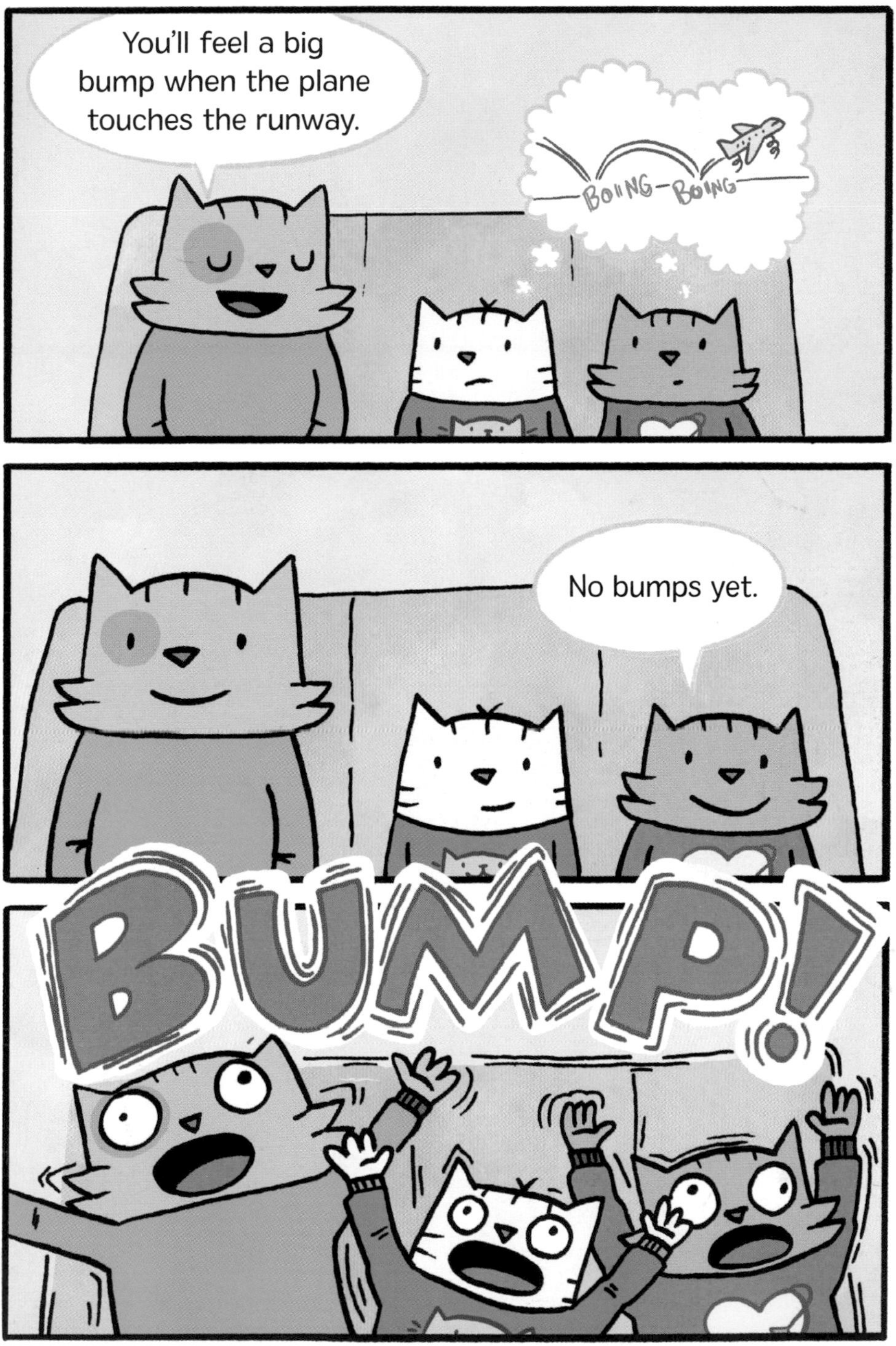
You'll feel a big bump when the plane touches the runway.
BOING-BOING
No bumps yet.
BUMP!

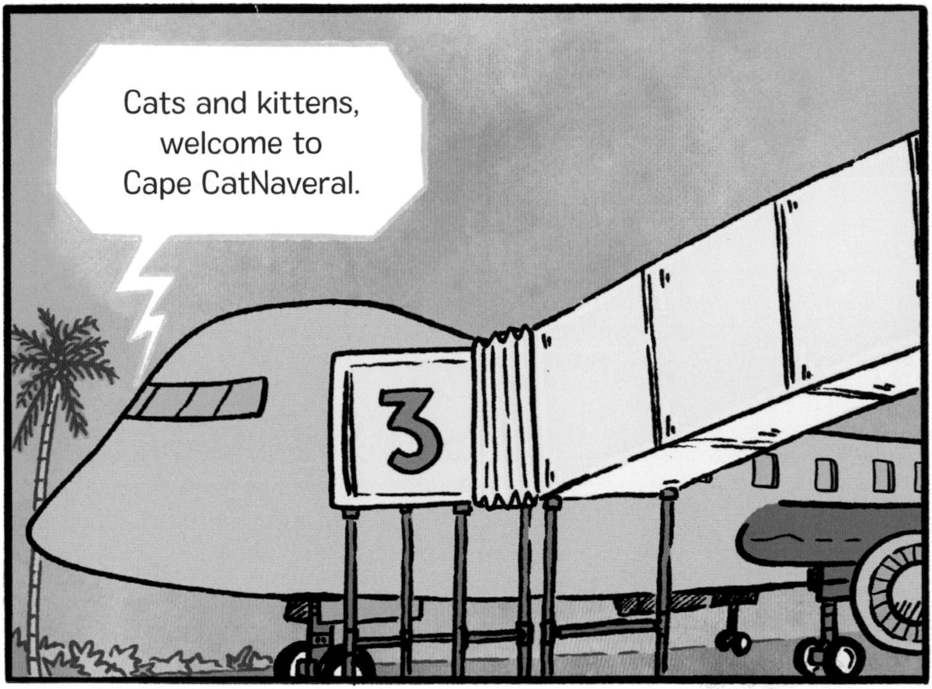
Cats and kittens, welcome to Cape CatNaveral.
3

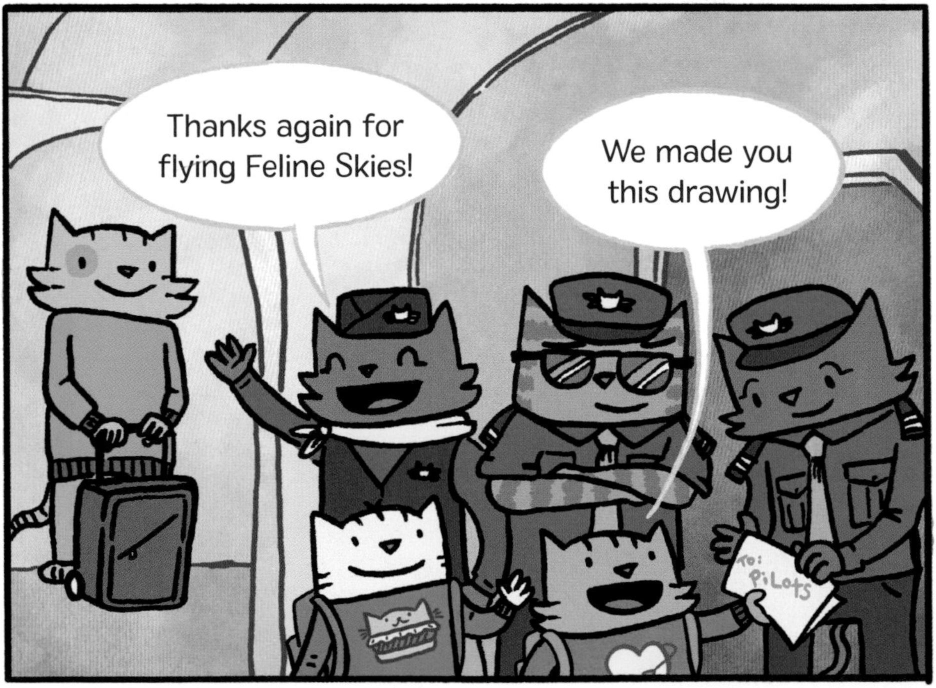
Thanks again for flying Feline Skies!
We made you this drawing!
To: PiLots

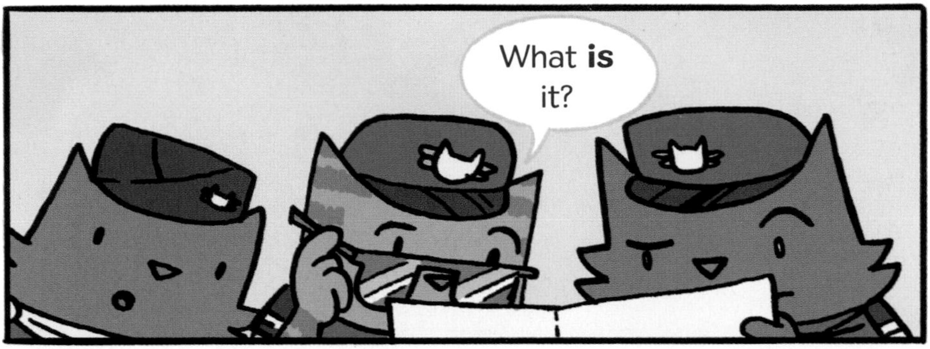
What **is** it?

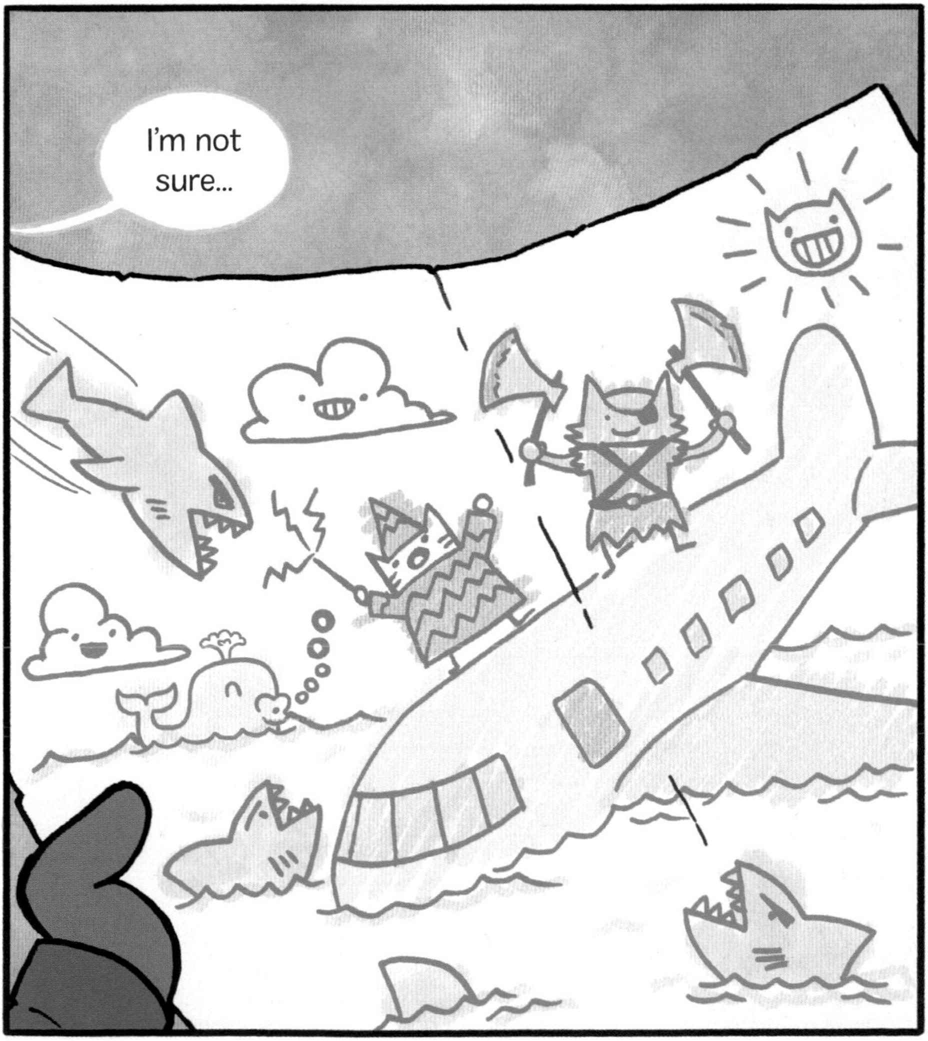
I'm not sure...

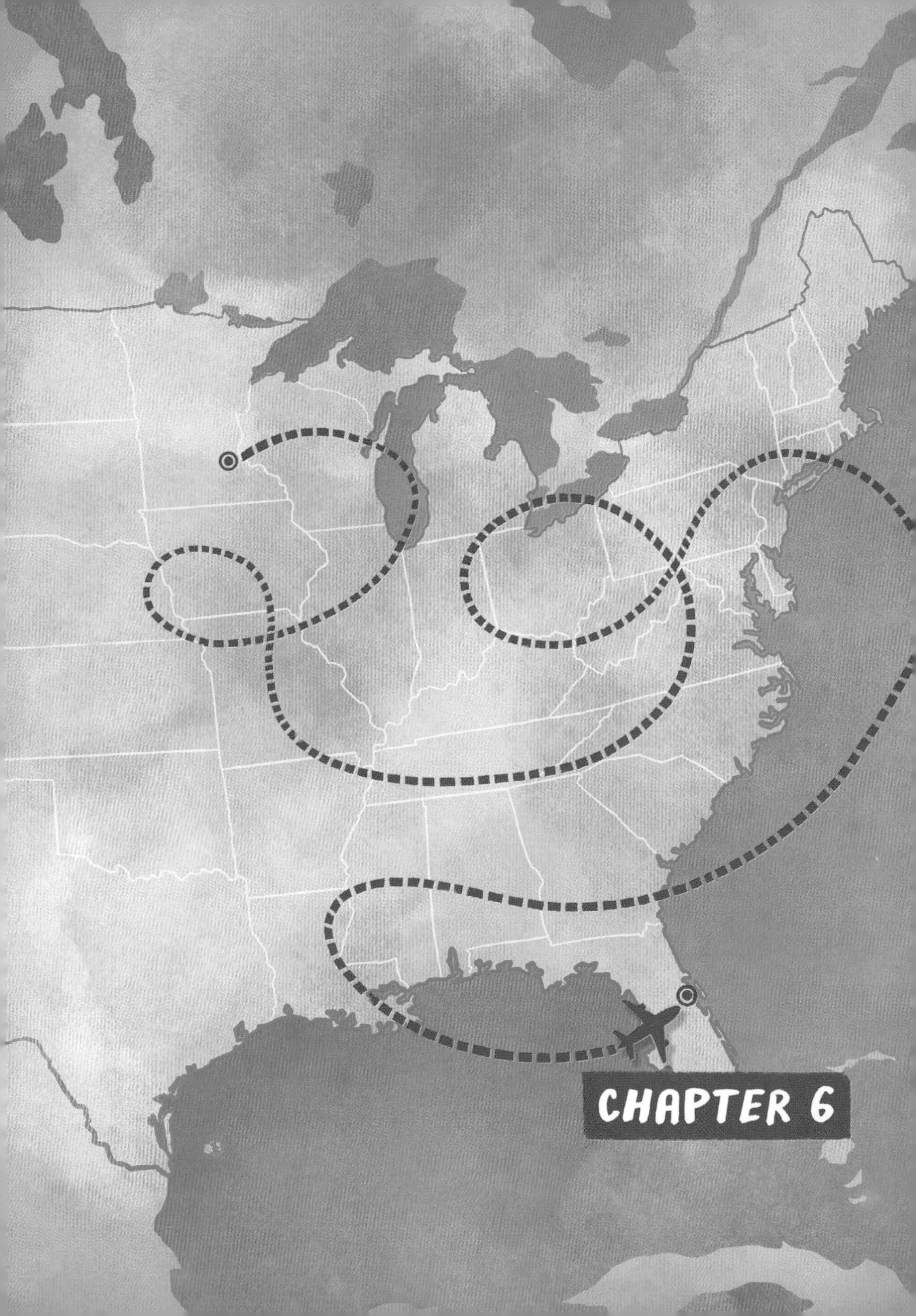

CHAPTER 6

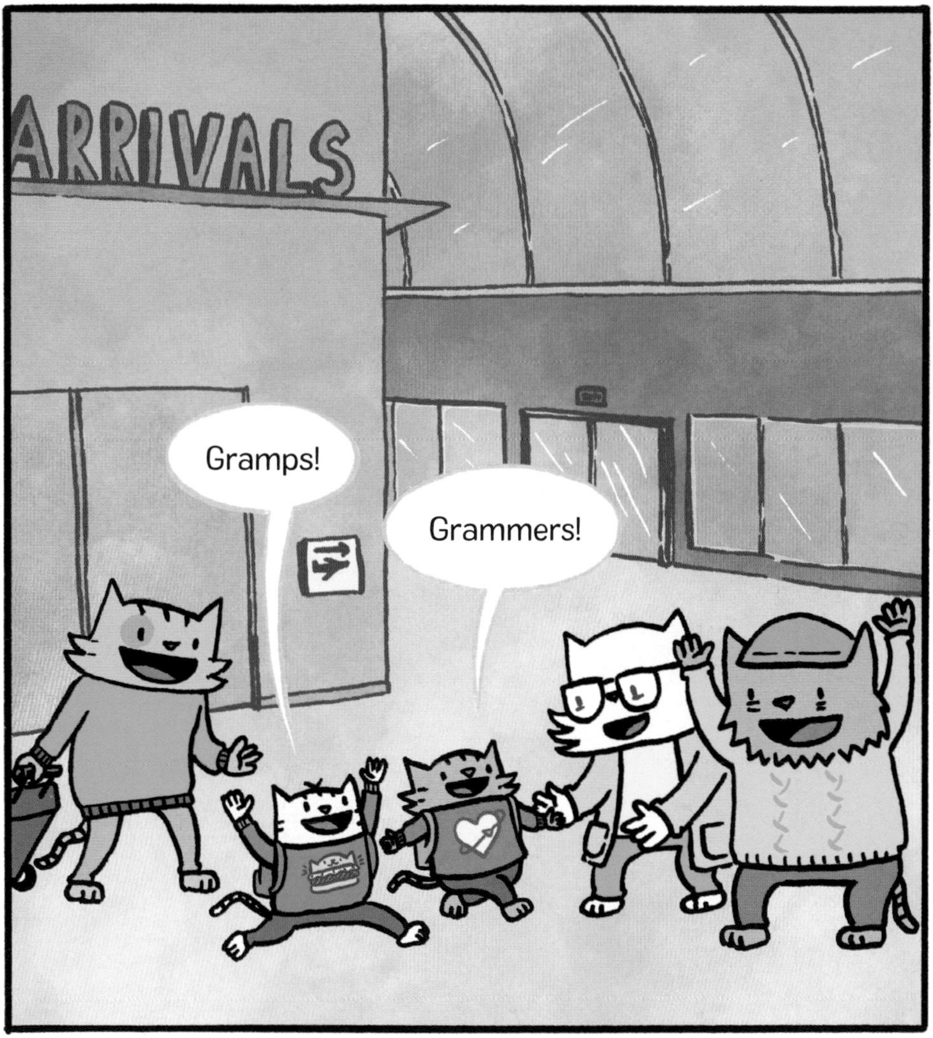
ARRIVALS
Gramps!
Grammers!

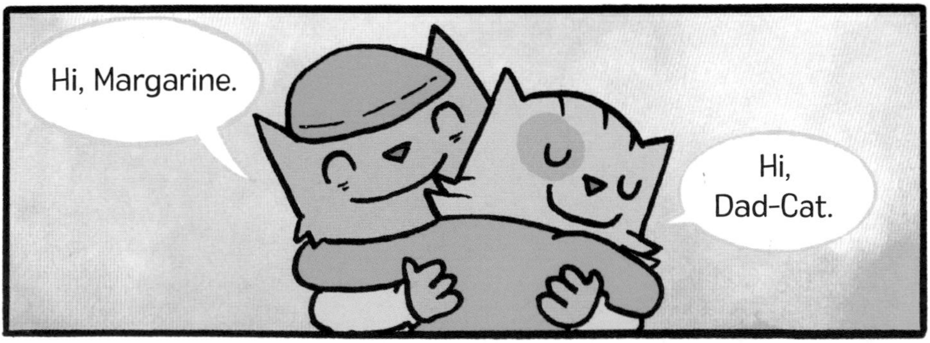
Hi, Margarine.
Hi, Dad-Cat.

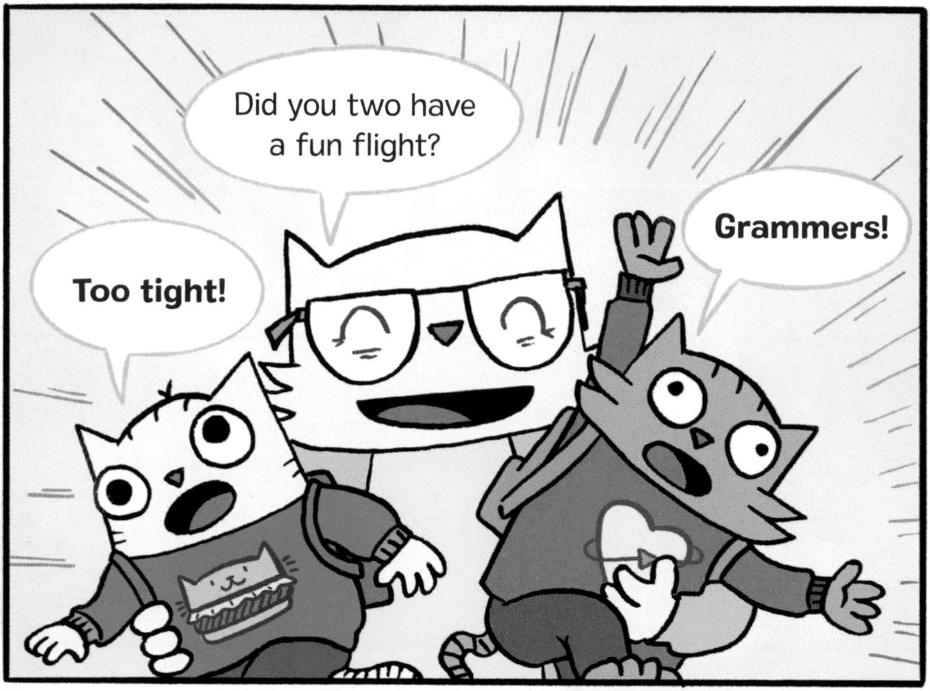
Did you two have a fun flight?
Too tight!
Grammers!

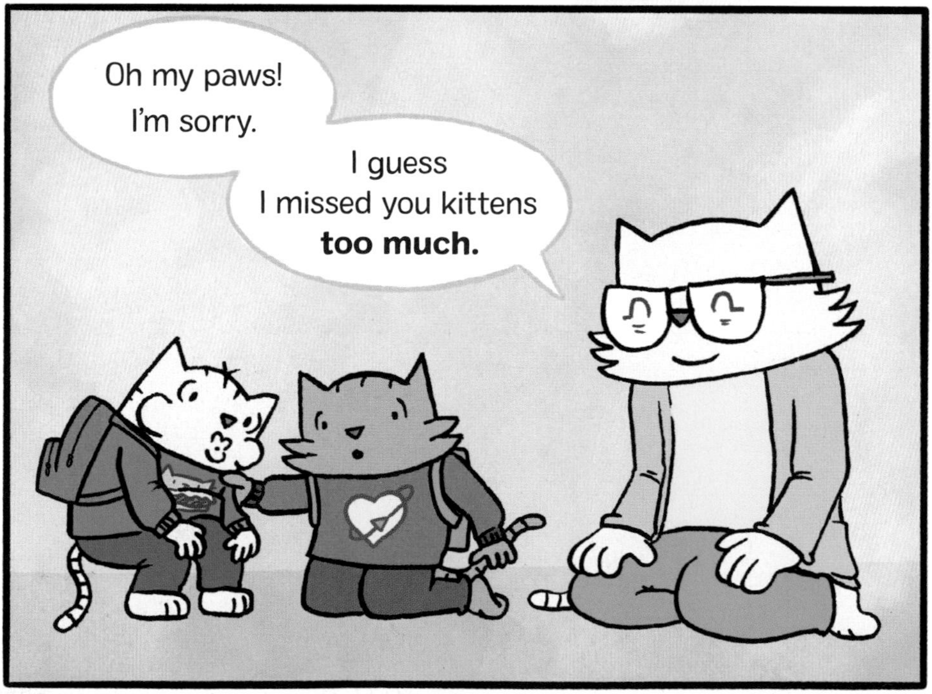
Oh my paws! I'm sorry.
I guess I missed you kittens **too much.**

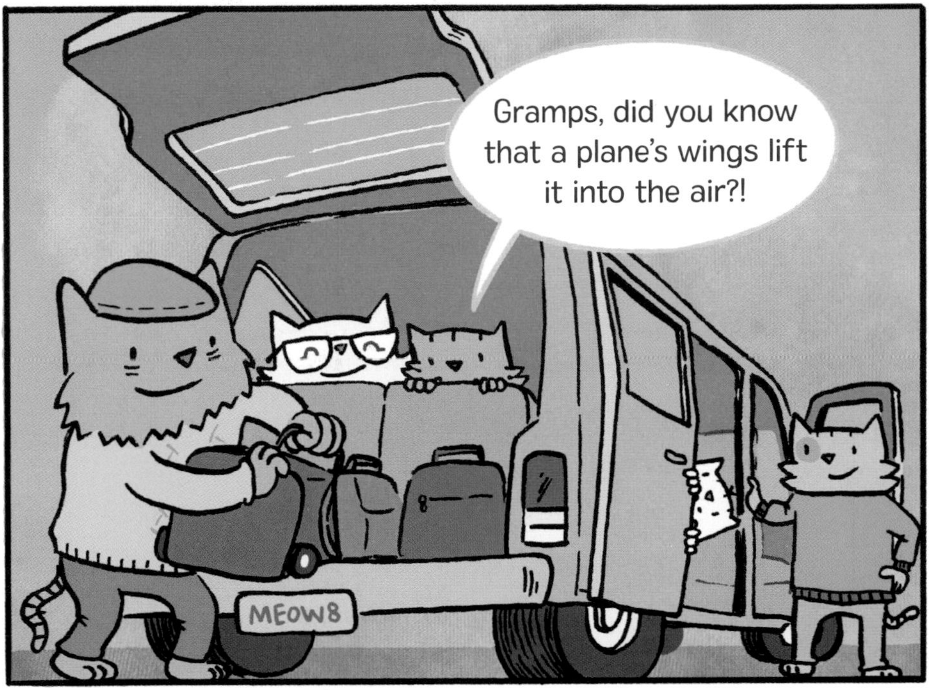
Gramps, did you know that a plane's wings lift it into the air?!
MEOW8

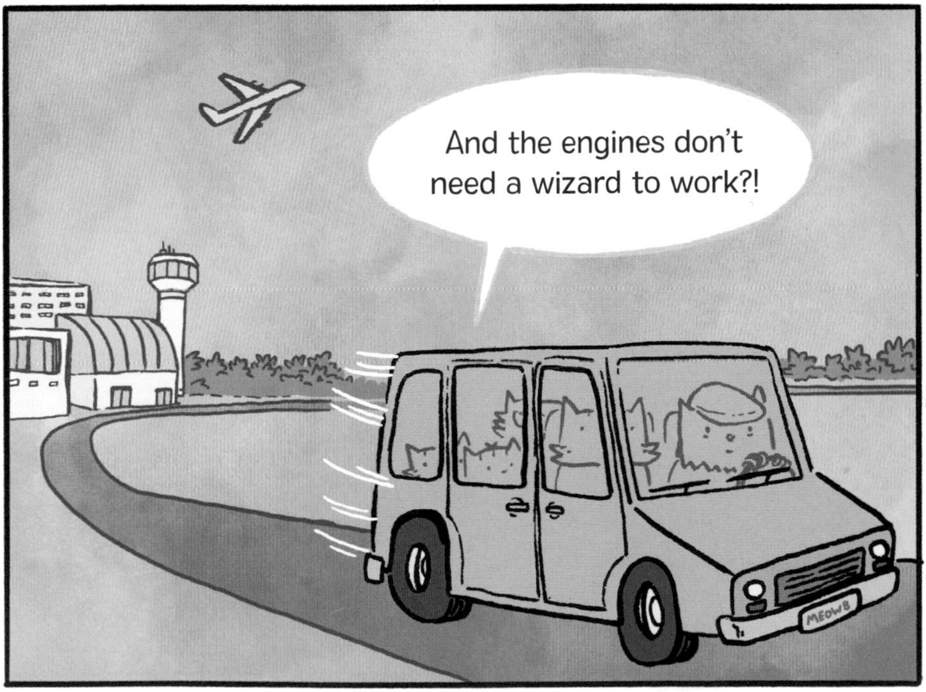
And the engines don't need a wizard to work?!
MEOW8

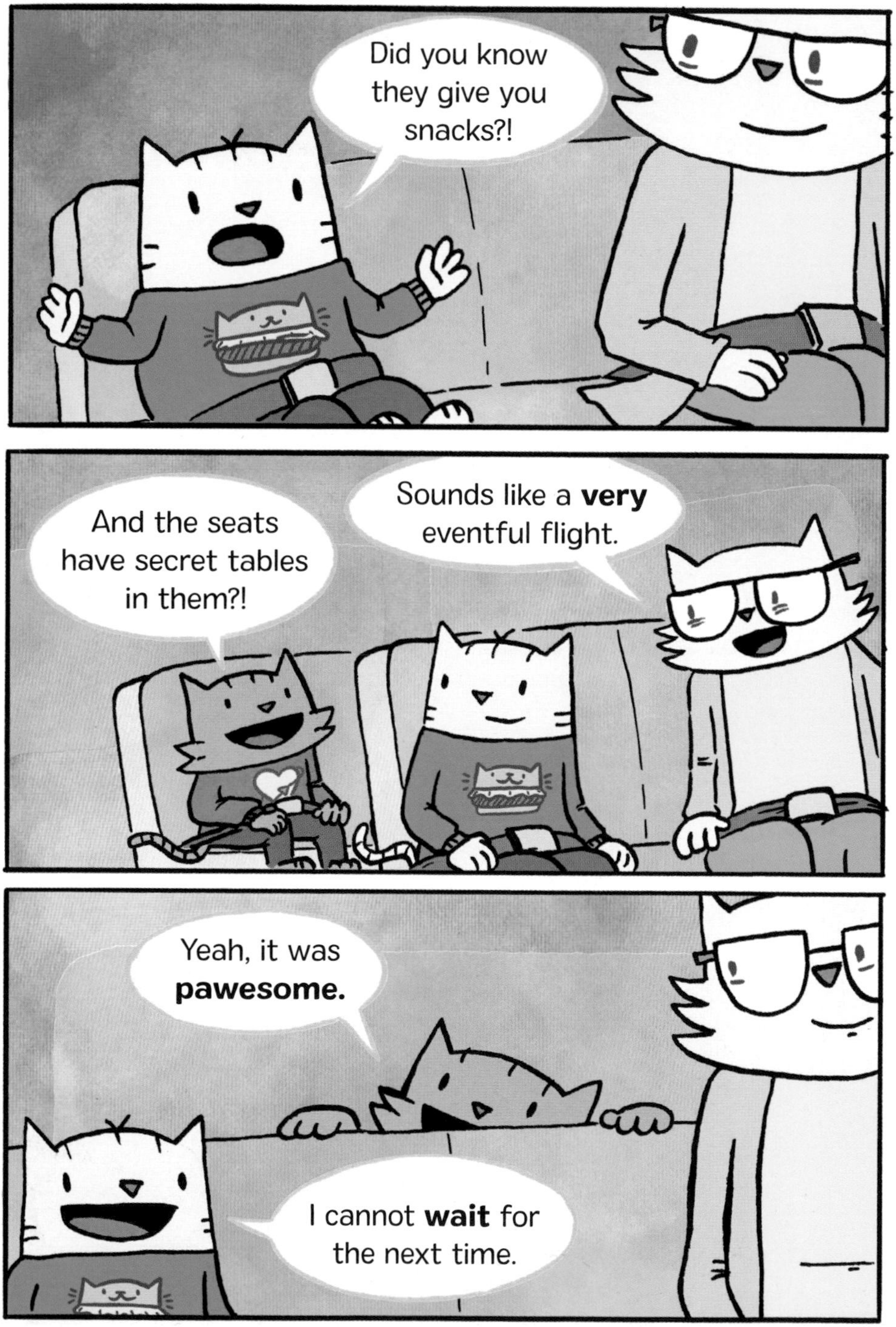
Did you know they give you snacks?!
And the seats have secret tables in them?!
Sounds like a **very** eventful flight.
Yeah, it was **pawesome.**
I cannot **wait** for the next time.

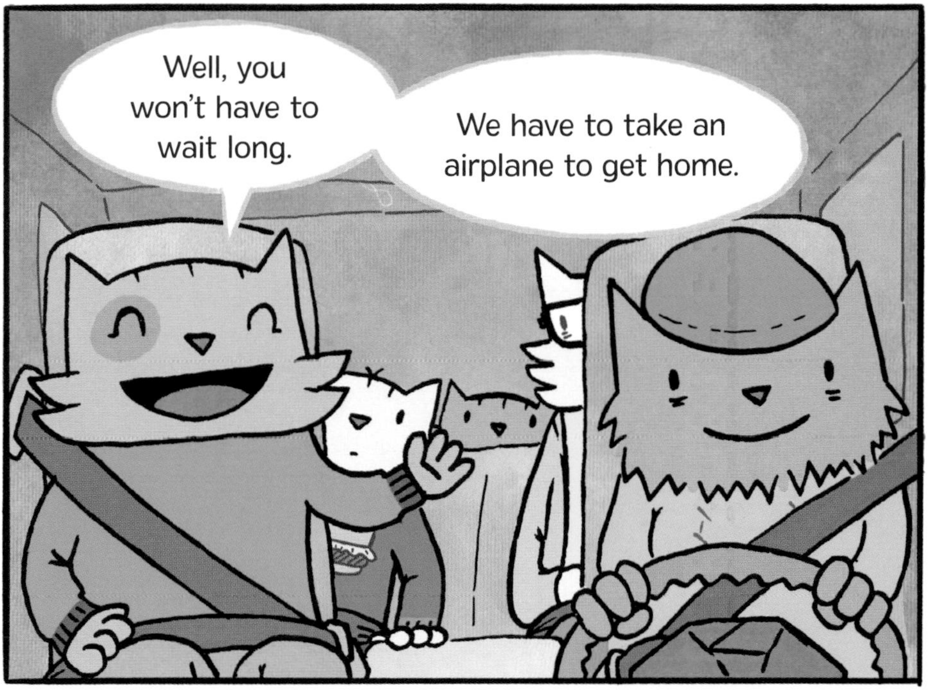
Well, you won't have to wait long.
We have to take an airplane to get home.

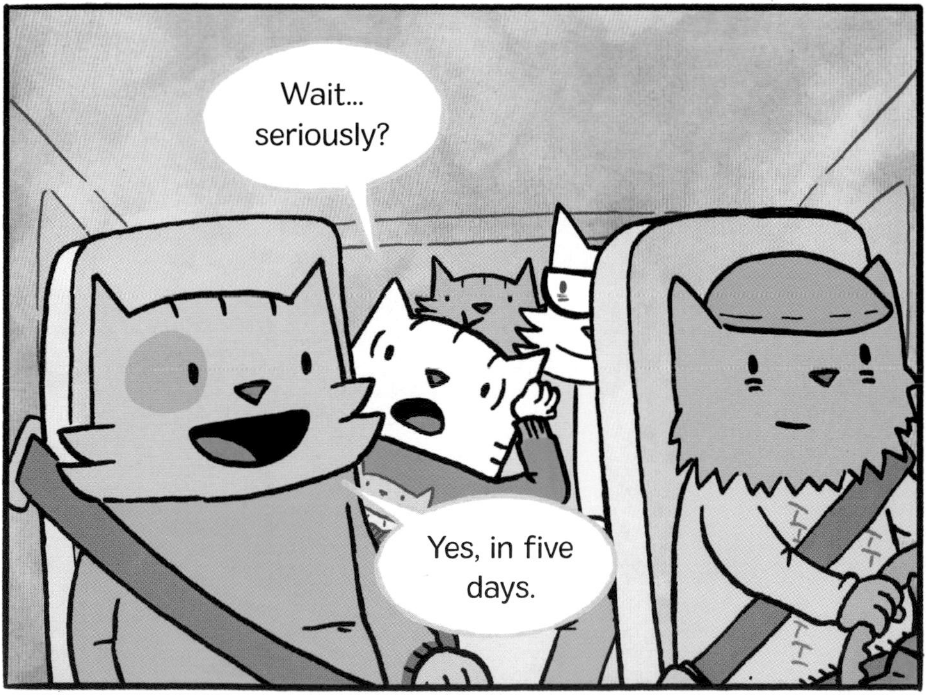
Wait... seriously?
Yes, in five days.

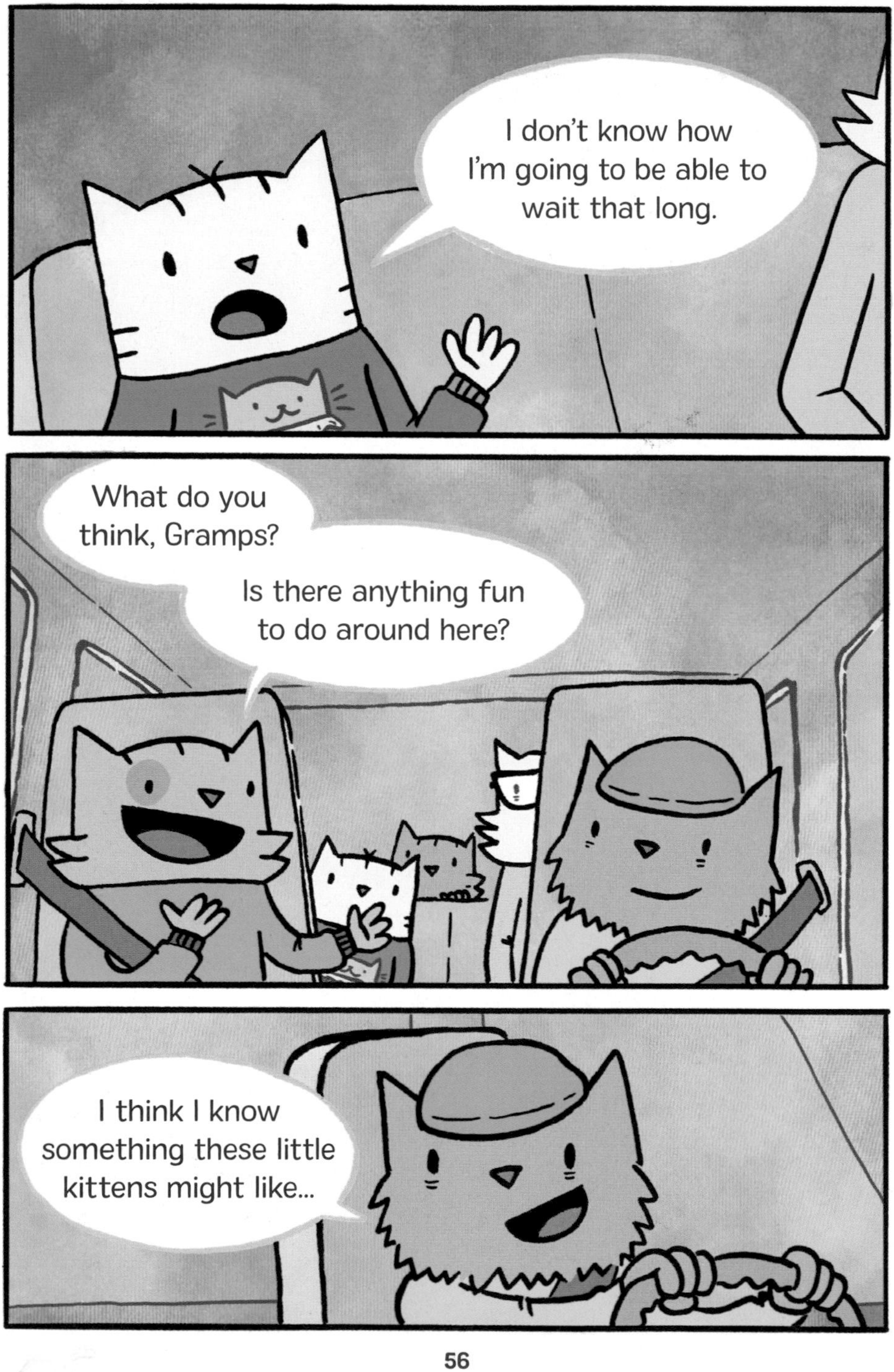
I don't know how I'm going to be able to wait that long.
What do you think, Gramps?
Is there anything fun to do around here?
I think I know something these little kittens might like...

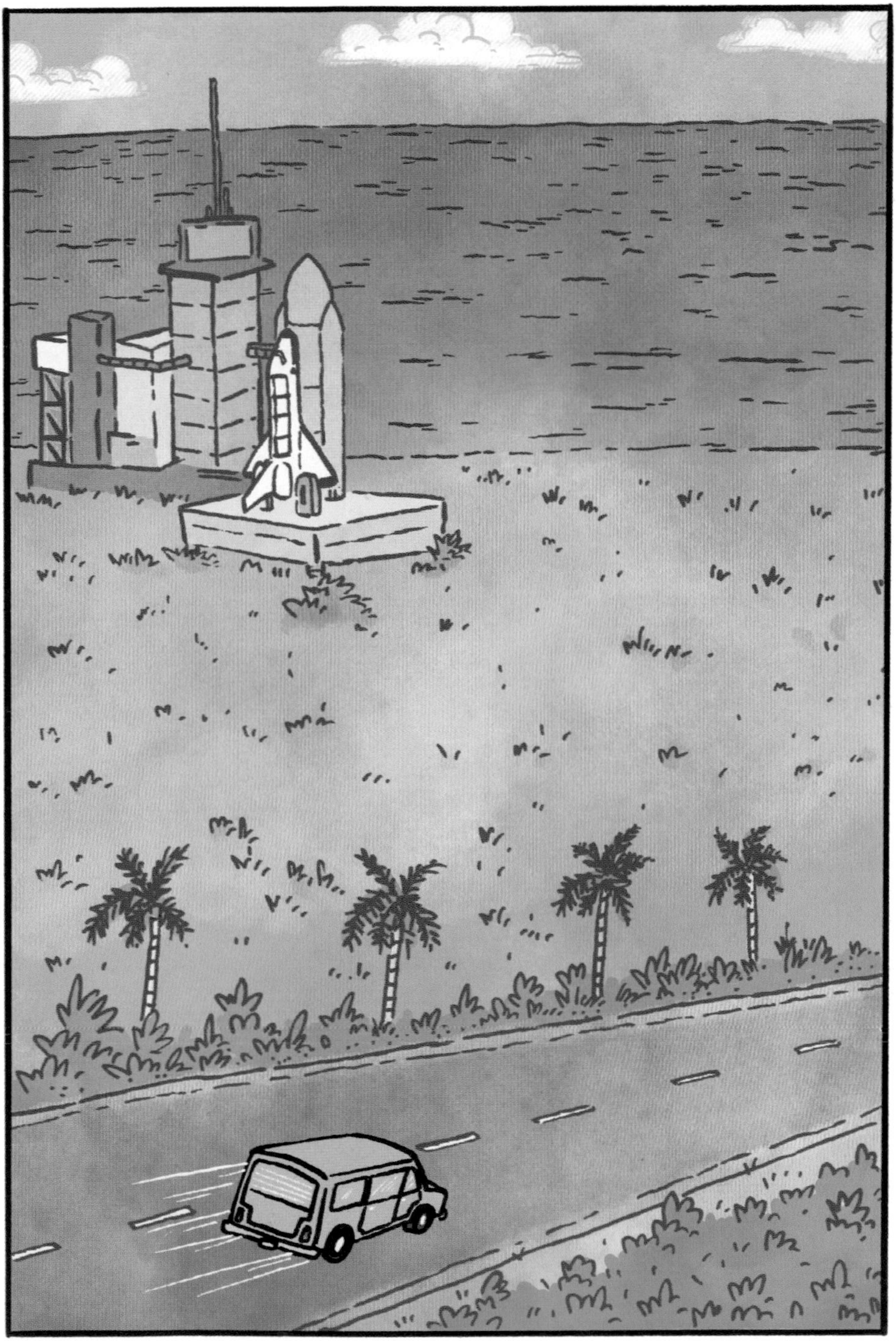

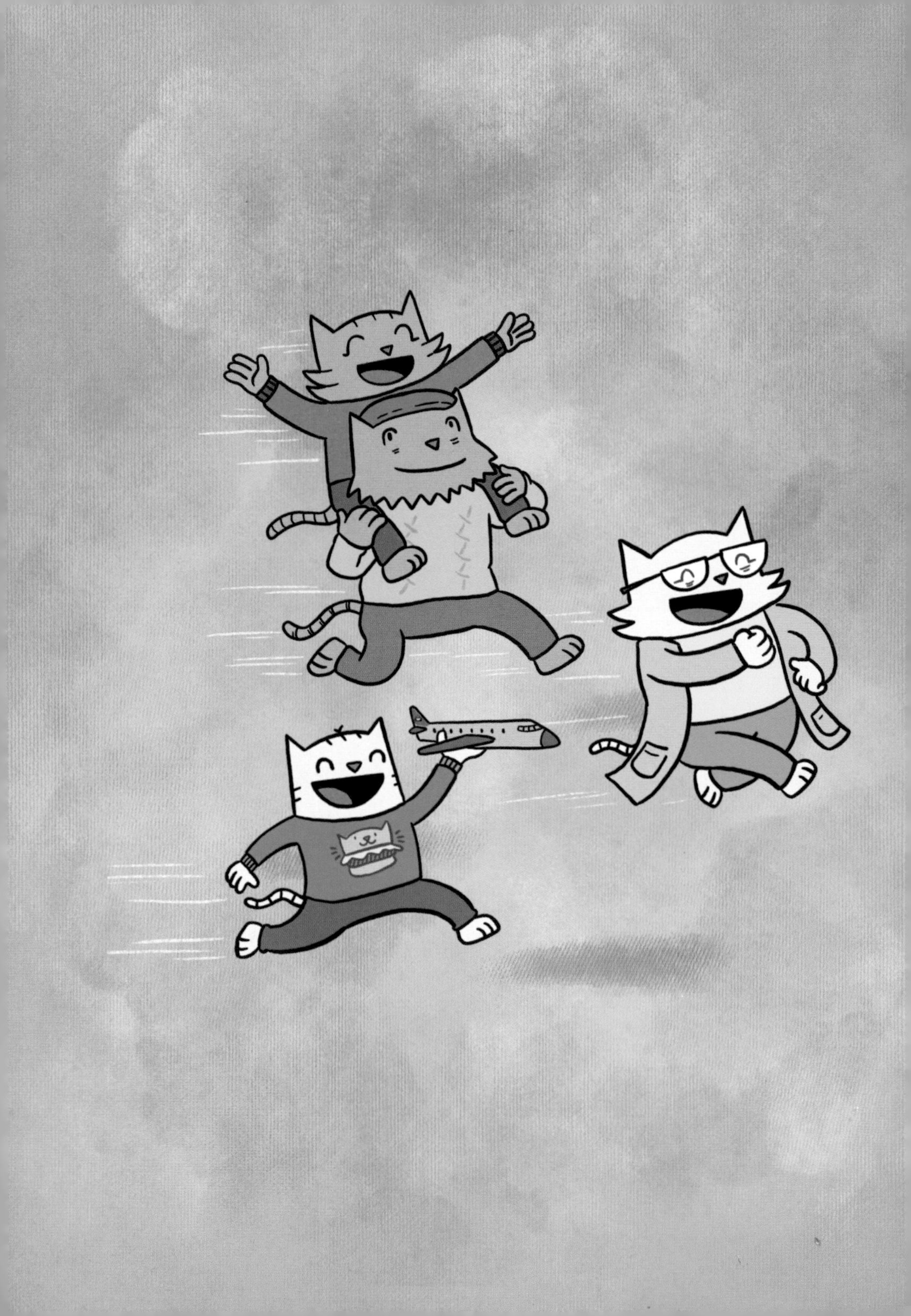

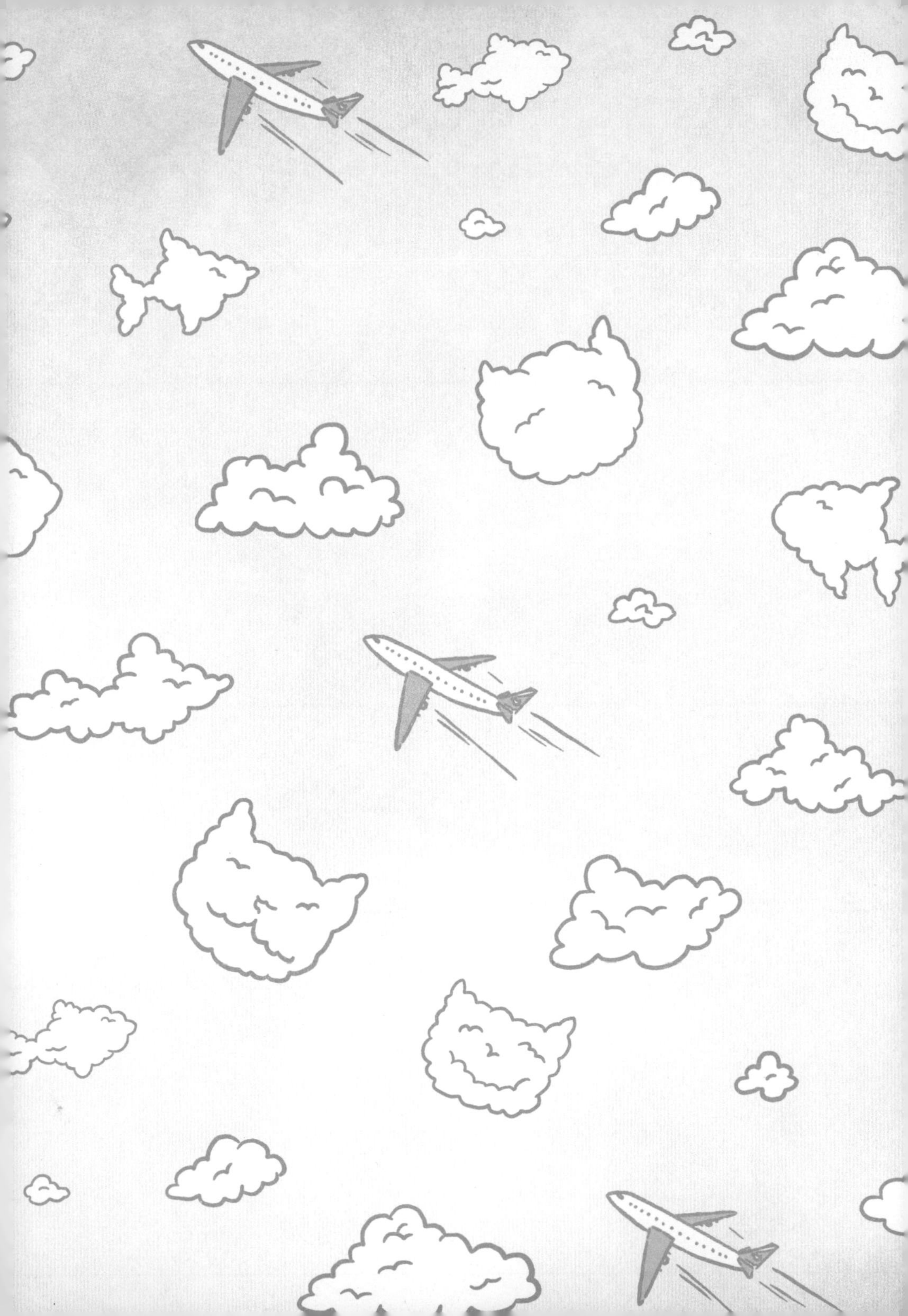